PRAISE FOR LUCY J. MADISON

"Lucy Madison's *A Recipe for Love* delivers a sizzling hot love story against a backdrop of luscious food and sexy cooking. Still reeling from the loss of her girlfriend and father, Danika is a woman on the precipice of a new life. And what a life it is, complete with a new home in a breathtaking landscape and meeting the complex and irresistible Finn."

— RANDI TRIANT, AUTHOR

"Lucy Madison's contemporary romance novel, *A Recipe for Love: A Lesbian Culinary Romance*, is a sheer delight to read. Madison's characters are credible and finely depicted, and her plot is fresh and engaging. And the food! Did I mention the food? The cooking lessons Danika signs up for are a marvel in themselves and the edibles she whips up in her new abode are mouth-watering for sure. Madison's second chance story is beautifully told, and I enjoyed every moment I spent getting to know Danika, Natalie and Finn. *A Recipe for Love: A Lesbian Culinary Romance* is most highly recommended."

— READERS' FAVORITE

"Set in the bucolic region of upstate NY, fyi for New Yorkers that is anywhere north of the Bronx, lol! 55 year old Danika has just retired with a full pension and is sitting on a gold mine, her parents home of 50 years. All is not good, she's facing a midlife crisis and her self-confidence is nil. Her partner of 20 years died 18 months ago, then her father died 11 months ago and she has been treading water ever since. With the help of her friend Natalie she is about to turn her life around. And none of it will be as easy as pie. A whirlwind of a book, with characters so vivid you will want to find a book club, STAT!, to talk about all the action that happens over the next 12 months to Danika, Finn, Natalie, Tony and Pete."

— ELAINE MULLIGAN-LYNCH

PRAISE FOR LUCY J. MADISON

"While this is categorized as a lesbian romance, there's actually a much bigger story going on here, and it was that element that really sucked me in."

— RACHEL WELLS, CURVE MAGAZINE

"*A Recipe for Love* is a well-crafted love story peppered with delicious scenes and fresh dialogue. The sweetness of this unique culinary adventure stays with the reader long after the story ends."

— MICKEY BRENT, AUTHOR

"*A Recipe For Love* by Lucy J. Madison is a heartwarming and, in a non-traditionally way, an uplifting romance novel with well-developed characterization and a storyline to compliment it."

— THE READING BUD

A RECIPE FOR LOVE

A LESBIAN CULINARY ROMANCE

LUCY J. MADISON

Labrador Publishing

Editor: Gabriella West

Cover Design: Lucy J. Madison

Labrador Publishing

24 W. Main St. Suite 330

Clinton, CT 06413

www.labradorpublishing.com

Printed in the United States of America

First Edition - October 10, 2018

"Great food is like great sex. The more you have, the more you want." – Gael Greene

For Julia and Louie

ACKNOWLEDGMENTS

Thank you to my fabulous beta readers Paula, Carmen, and Marsha for your honesty, time, and support. Your feedback was invaluable.

I'm very lucky to have found my editor, Gabriella West, who is nit-picky in the best possible way. Thank you for your attention to detail.

Special thanks to Julez Weinberg for allowing me to include some of her incredible cocktails from her book *The Essential Mixologist*.

Thanks to Allie and Ilene at Roux Provincetown for hosting an incredible book launch party during Women's Week featuring some of the recipes from this book, and for your continued support of artists and writers.

Thank you to the incomparable food critic and author Gael Greene for allowing permission to use your famous quote to kick off this culinary romance.

Special thanks to the Golden Crown Literary Society for your support of lesbian literature and for providing a space where authors and readers can connect and talk about the lesbian books that we love.

Thanks to bestselling author Lynn Ames for taking the time to offer me guidance and advice. I truly appreciate it!

Thank you to Michele Karlsberg for being my publicity guru, and for your ongoing and continued support of my writing career. I am blessed to have you in my life.

Finally, thank you to all my readers and fans around the world. I write because I love to tell stories, but your support keeps me going. I.V. now and always.

CHAPTER ONE

Danika had waited long enough. She peeked into the oven at the cheesy soufflé and knew by looking at its height that it was perfectly cooked. She removed the round, white porcelain ramekin from the oven, gently placing the perfectly risen, browned soufflé on the worn kitchen counter. This soufflé had been a staple for her over the years, but the excitement of an impeccably risen soufflé never got old. Danika thought about grabbing her cell phone to take a photo before the soufflé fell, but she decided to pick up her fork instead.

After a few sublime mouthfuls of the cheesy, airy, eggy goodness, she rested her elbows on the kitchen counter and looked around. Birds chirped outside. Early summer sunlight streamed through the kitchen windows, a blessing after the brutal New England winter, even though the sunlight highlighted the dust on every surface. *Now what?* she thought to herself. Danika had nothing to do. Her first official day of retirement arrived on this first Monday in May. She had worked one job or another since she was sixteen years old. Thirty-nine years later, at the ripe old age of fifty-five, she had nowhere to be and no idea what to do with the rest of the day, let alone the rest of her life. It wasn't unsettling, it was downright terrifying.

Danika always expected to be settled by the time she retired. She'd imagined having a partner with whom to cook, talk about books and movies, visit art galleries, and travel. She envisaged being partnered. Prepared. Somehow, the opposite had proven to be true. Danika never thought that receiving an A.A.R.P. card would cause near-physical discomfort. She was alone, living in her parents' old house in Nyack, New York, ill-prepared for retired life.

Cooking always soothed her nerves, hence the cheddar cheese soufflé at nine-fifteen in the morning. But now that the dishes were clean, and the soufflé was almost entirely polished off, her eyes scanned the dated knotty-pine cabinets of the kitchen she grew up in and felt like a total and utter failure. How on earth did she wind up back here, in this 1970s time-warp house, of all places?

Danika sat down on the window seat, immediately soothed by the warm sun. She sighed and looked out the window that needed cleaning at the overgrown garden, requiring tending and pruning. Add that to the list of jobs she did not want to think about. Not now, not ever. The responsibility of it all tightened like a rogue vine around her neck, suffocating her. She closed her eyes and saw a smaller version of herself running through the kitchen, out the back door, grabbing her banana bike, so popular when she was a kid, on the run, off to the water or the woods, or both. The fleeting memory felt like yesterday, like last week, like a lifetime ago.

She tried to think back to when she was young and had dreams for her life. She couldn't remember a single one. Her whole life, she'd been taking things day-by-day, and that had apparently gotten her nowhere.

Bringing herself back to the present, Danika leaned over and grabbed a stack of mail. Tearing open the manila envelope, she stared hard at a copy of her father's death certificate and felt absolutely nothing. She should have felt sadness or loss, but she felt neither. Too much water had passed under that bridge over the years. Theirs wasn't a happy father-daughter relationship, and never really had been. She re-folded the certificate and placed it back in the envelope for safe-keeping. The first had been lost in the mess of her parents' house. Her father had died almost a year ago, and the place looked virtually the same as it had when she was nine years old in 1972. Even down to the puke-green rotary phone mounted on the kitchen wall, its twenty-foot cord hanging on the warped, rust-colored linoleum floor. She'd been living here for eleven months since her father's death, hating every moment of it. Eleven months! What was she still doing here? She hated this place. Yet, here she was, right back where she started, without a clue as to what to do next. The pressure of it all weighed on her chest, making it feel as though she was slowly being suffocated to death. She tried to take a deep breath but felt stifled. She nearly wheezed out a shallow breath, sounding more like a life-long smoker than herself.

To make matters worse, she'd had her annual mammogram last week. The doctor didn't like the way the mammogram looked, so he'd sent her for an ultrasound. She'd been waiting three days for the results. When a doctor tells you that you have dense breasts, and they potentially saw a spot, and you have a long and painful history with cancer, you tend to panic. Danika was a step away from full-blown panic.

Before she could make herself feel any more pitiful and anxious, her cell phone rang. She picked up on the second ring.

"Hello?"

"Are you going to open your front door, or do I need to break in?" a familiar mock-annoyed voice asked.

"You're here? I didn't hear the bell," replied Danika. She stood, peeking toward the front door.

"Dammit, Dan, that doorbell's been broken for fifteen years."

Danika ended the call and walked through the kitchen to the front hall. She unlatched the chain and opened the heavy wooden door. Her best friend, Natalie, stood in the doorway, her eyebrows furrowed into a cross. Natalie always looked as if she had just come from, or was headed to, the gym. Danika barely recalled a time when Natalie didn't wear sneakers, sweats, yoga pants, or some combination thereof. Her friend always reminded her of the Energizer Bunny, short, compact, and bursting with energy. Natalie was at least five or six inches shorter than Danika, but her big personality always made up for her diminutive size.

"It's about damned time," she sniped as she walked into the house carrying a brown bag, right past Danika.

"What are you doing here?" Danika asked.

"I brought breakfast. How do bagels and lox sound?" Natalie made herself at home in the kitchen and immediately added both noise and energy to the quiet room. Natalie moved with a clean efficiency, pulling out dishes and forks, unpacking the bagels, lox, red onion, capers, and lemon. The pungent smell of lox and red onion immediately filled the room.

Danika looked a little guilty. "That sounds fabulous, but I'm stuffed. I made a cheese soufflé."

At the word *soufflé*, Natalie froze and looked up at Danika, her eyebrows raised. "Did you say soufflé?" She shifted from sneaker to sneaker like a starting gun would go off any second.

Danika laughed, then nodded. "I did."

Natalie looked around. "Well, where the hell is it?"

Danika patted her chubby belly and smiled.

"You ate the whole thing?" Natalie's voice hung on the word "whole" for added emphasis as her eyes widened in surprise.

"The whole thing." At the sight of Natalie's raised eyebrows, Danika continued, "What? It's mostly air anyway." She poured a cup of coffee into a chipped mug and handed it to Natalie. She poured another cup for herself. Danika sat down at the brown Formica island in the kitchen on a rickety old oak bar stool that creaked and groaned every time she shifted her weight.

"Any big revelations on your first official day of retirement?" Natalie asked as she sliced a bagel and dropped it into the toaster.

Danika peeled off a small piece of lox and stuffed it into her mouth. The saltiness immediately made her mouth water. "Yeah. Two. I'm never going to be skinny again, and I don't know what I want to be when I grow up. Make that three. I don't miss my parents at all, and I'm feeling pretty guilty about that. I should, right? I should feel sadness or mourn or whatever, but the thing is, I don't really mind that they're gone, except I'm pissed they left me with this mess of a house." Danika tried to keep the anger from rising up like bile in her throat.

Natalie laughed and ran her fingers through her cropped black hair that was beginning to turn gray at the temples. Danika always wished she could wear her hair that way, but when she went through her G.I. Jane phase and cut it all off, it wasn't pretty. Instead of looking sharp and sexy, Danika looked oddly like a Muppet. Natalie had made her promise never to cut her hair like that again. Danika self-consciously adjusted the ponytail that she'd slept in.

The bagel popped up out of the toaster a golden brown. Natalie proceeded to methodically build her bagel with a layer of cream cheese, then capers, then lox. She covered the lox with thinly sliced red onion and wafer-thin sliced tomato. Natalie squeezed lemon over the top and proceeded to take a bite while sitting down beside Danika. In between chewing, she said, "Dan, take some time to relax. We both know your parents weren't exactly there for you. Plus, it's been a year for your dad and what, like ten for your mom? You've had a hell of a year. Now that your dad is gone, you can decide what you want to do with this place."

"I know. All I do is look around at what needs to be done inside and out, and I don't know if I have the energy for it." Danika's chest heaved in a big sigh staring at the overgrown garden again.

"Or if you even want to, right?"

"Right. How much have I always hated this house?"

"The question isn't how much; it's more like how long. Let's see; I met you when we were in second grade. That was forty-eight years ago. For as long as I've known you, you've wanted out of this place, and I can't say I blame you."

Natalie sighed again and sipped her coffee. The two stared absentmindedly out the window in a companionable silence that came from so many years of friendship, broken only by Natalie's chewing.

"You can sell the house, Dan. Sell it and do something you want to do. First, you took care of Angela, then you took care of your father. Maybe now it's time for you to take care of yourself."

Danika nodded half-heartedly. "What's wrong? I know that look," Natalie prompted.

"I still haven't heard back from the doctor about the ultrasound." Danika unsuccessfully tried to keep the worry out of her voice.

Natalie squeezed her arm. "I'm sure it'll be fine. No news is good news. If there was a problem, they probably would've called back right away. You can't sit around and worry about it. I'm serious. You've got to take care of yourself and live a little."

"Yeah," Danika responded meekly. She knew her friend was right. Danika never really had a problem admitting things to herself. But over the years, she developed an inability or unwillingness to move, to change, to risk, to live outside her comfort zone. Even if that comfort zone wasn't where she wanted to be, the routine of the status quo was always more appealing. The thing is, she hadn't always been like that. She used to be a risk-taker. Like the time she flung herself off the side of the Calf Pen in Lake George while Natalie looked in in horror. They were what, fifteen? Sixteen? She relived the rush as she flew through the air, hurtling downwards toward the clear water below.

"I'm stuck. I know I'm stuck, and too old to start over. Look at me I'm not exactly a spring chicken. The mere thought of starting over for the third time is too much to deal with." Danika picked a red piece of lint off her gray cargo shorts. "Do you remember when we snuck off to Calf Pen in Lake George and I jumped off the edge? What was the name of that place?"

"Yeah. Calf Pen I think it's called. I was terrified you'd hit your head on the side," Natalie said in between bites.

"But I did it, didn't I? I jumped."

"Where is this coming from? That's ancient history," Natalie looked puzzled.

"I was so adventurous then," Danika said quietly while gazing again out the windows. "Something happened, and I changed."

"Hon, it's called life. We both know you would have left Angela years ago if she didn't get sick first. She was never the one for you. But, you did the right thing by caring for her through cancer, and I agree it wasn't fair that your dad got sick right after Angela died. You haven't had a moment to yourself in like six years. Of course, it's going to be uncomfortable. Change always is."

"Yeah, but you're much better with change than I am. You embrace it more. I run from it." Danika sighed again into her coffee cup.

"Will you stop with all the sighing? You're sucking all the oxygen out of the room." She paused, staring intently at Danika's forlorn expression. "Okay! I have a brilliant idea!" Natalie jumped up and shook the bagel crumbs off her virtually flat chest. She rummaged through the junk drawer in the kitchen for a pen and paper, then sat back down next to Danika.

"Let's make a list."

Danika scoffed. "Of what? All the crap I have to do around here?"

"No, of all the things you always wanted to do but never got around to. I mean fun stuff—not stuff like *you have to clean the garage.*"

"Seriously?" Danika groaned and laid her head in her arms over the countertop.

"Seriously. Come on. Play along. You can say anything. Don't think about how much something costs or how unrealistic it might be. Throw some things out there."

"This is a terrible game, and you're a terrible friend."

"Quit your bitching. You know you love me." Natalie smacked Danika on the back as if to push fresh air into her friend's lungs like someone does when attempting to save a drowning person.

"Making a list will not change my life," Danika protested, her eyebrows knitted into a "v" on her forehead.

"Ahh, so we admit to wanting to change our life, then?" Natalie retorted.

"Nat, I'm too old to change. By this point in life, a person is who a person is. I'm not going to wake up and look like Salma Hayek tomorrow morning, no matter how many lists I make."

Danika wiped her clammy hands on her shorts. Something about this conversation made her nervous and uneasy. The idea of wanting more and going out there to get it felt almost too real, and made her feel the tiniest bit alive. For a moment, she could've been standing in front of an open airplane door 13,000 feet in the air ready to jump into the great blue beyond rather than inside this horribly claustrophobic kitchen thinking about her future with Natalie, all while she waited for a call back from the doctor about her ultrasound results. Having breast cancer wasn't exactly on her bucket list.

CHAPTER TWO

Fifteen minutes later, Natalie leaned back on the bar stool with a smug smile on her face. "See, this was a great exercise. Look at all of these exciting things!" She rapped the paper with her pen for added emphasis.

Danika interjected, "That I'll never get around to doing. Do we really think it's realistic for me to hike in Tibet? I can barely climb a flight of stairs without passing out."

"Don't be such a pessimist. Are a few things possibly a little out of reach? Maybe. Big deal. You spent all your energy making sure Angela and your dad had everything they needed that you stopped thinking about what you needed. Saying some things out loud that you'd want to experience is an achievement. It's a start, is all I'm saying."

"You're right. I know you're right. The first thing I need to do is to figure out what the hell to do with myself every day."

"Well, the good news is you don't have to deliver other people's mail anymore!"

Danika didn't perk up at the reminder. "Yeah, but I enjoyed walking my route every day. It kept me outside. I listened to audiobooks, saw people. You know I did some of my best thinking while walking that same route each day."

"Dan, you had that route for like a hundred years."

"Don't be dramatic. It was only thirty."

Natalie whipped out her phone and punched in a few numbers on the calculator app. "Only thirty, she says. As if it's no big deal that you worked at the same job for 10,950 days. In a row. 10,950! With hardly a sick day taken."

"Geez. It's not like I was doing brain surgery all that time. I walked around and stuffed paper into mailboxes. It's not like it was an emotionally or intellectually taxing job."

"That's the thing about you, Dan. You stick. You stuck to that job for thirty years because it was stable. Hell, you stuck to me like glue, and I can't seem to get rid of you." Natalie winked and continued. "You stuck with Angela for twenty years because you made a commitment you weren't going to break, and toward the end, she needed you more than you needed her. You stuck with your father until the day he died, even though we both know that he didn't give two shits about you. He certainly didn't deserve any of your love or devotion, but you gave it to him anyway. You ran away once when we were eleven years old for like six hours. Do you remember that?"

Danika nodded.

"Six hours. Then you came back because you were worried about your mom needing help with dinner. And we both know she couldn't cook to save her life. You've always done the right thing, the good thing. You paid your dues, babe. Now live a little before your living is through."

"That's awfully morbid." Danika frowned.

"It's not morbid. It's the truth. We're not getting any younger. You've lived almost your whole life doing for other people. Not once have I ever really seen you be a little selfish. It's not in your DNA." Natalie checked her watch and quickly jumped up, scraping the oak bar stool on the linoleum floor. "Shit. I've got to run. Suzie tasked me with grocery shopping, and if I don't get around to it because I hung out with you all day, she'll smother me with a pillow tonight after I fall asleep."

"You're a good wife." Danika said, smiling at her friend. Natalie and Suzie had been married for over thirty years. It was love at first sight. They raised two beautifully successful children who were now contributing positively to the world, whom Danika loved like the surrogate aunt she was. Danika sometimes felt a little jealous of the rich life Natalie and Suzie created together. Danika always wanted a partner like that, but it hadn't been in the cards for her. "Go. I don't want to get you in trouble," she replied, trying to sound chipper.

As the two walked toward the front door, Natalie said, "Call me as soon as you hear from the doctor. And, seriously, take a look at that list and see if there are one or two realistic things you can do now to try something new, and get out there a little bit. Think about the house. There's nothing wrong with selling it. I'm sure Suzie can help you get a great price. The market is hot here, and she is the best agent in town!"

"Okay, okay. I'll take a look. Get out of here. Thanks for coming by today. You always know when I need you." Danika hugged her friend and felt jealous for a moment of Natalie's tight, compact body that looked virtually the same now as it had when they were in their twenties. She stood in the doorway, watching Natalie walk down the overgrown front path to her Prius. Natalie waved as she hopped in the car. Danika waved back then closed front door. For a moment, she leaned against the front door and stared back into the house as if the house had just sucked out whatever remaining energy she possessed.

After tidying up the kitchen, Danika picked up the list she and Natalie had worked on. She stared at it for a moment or two before crumpling it into a ball and tossing it in the garbage.

Danika knew deep in her gut she did not want to stay here. The house held too many memories of her parents fighting, of her father throwing her out when she was eighteen because he'd caught her kissing Natalie. That had been her first kiss with another woman. All these years later, and the memory of that moment crackled inside of her.

That felt like a thousand years ago. They were kids, beginning to figure out who they were, but the pain of her father's immediate scorn stung as if it had happened yesterday. It was funny the things you remembered about awkward moments. Her father wore an orange golf shirt tucked into khaki pants, along with a beat-up pair of docksiders. She remembered thinking, as he screamed at her that she would go to hell for being an abomination to God and to their family, that he looked like an idiot wearing a golf shirt when he had never even picked up a golf club in his life. As spittle flew from her father's lips— landing on her, the coffee table, the shag rug, she'd wondered if he wore the golf shirt to make himself seem more pretentious than he already was.

Years later, when she cared for her father as he wasted away from stomach cancer, she'd wanted to bring up that moment, to find some closure for all of it, but each time she tried to broach the subject of their difficult past or even bring up Angela's name, her father pretended to be sleeping. Ultimately Danika let it go. They both found a space to co-exist where they never acknowledged the past, but didn't talk about anything of substance either. It wasn't ideal, but self-preservation sometimes creates odd behaviors.

Her parents never accepted her life choices. They'd made that entirely clear over the years during several knock-down, drag-out arguments. They were staunch Italian Catholics who believed Danika would go to hell for preferring women. Truthfully, Danika probably never would have come out to her parents if they hadn't caught her making out with Natalie. It would have been far more comfortable on all of them if she'd been able to keep that part of her hidden from their judgmental view. It had taken her years of therapy to come to terms with her sexuality to ultimately realize there was nothing wrong with her for being sexually attracted to other women. It also took her the better part of twenty years to realize that she did not need her parents' approval for her actions and choices. She never received that approval anyway. Danika tried to calculate the money spent on therapy for herself, losing count somewhere in the thousands.

She also thought back to the last time she saw her mother alive. Danika recalled seeing her mother grocery shopping in the local market, squeezing cantaloupes while Danika was headed to another aisle to buy beer. She remembered watching her mother methodically pick up a melon, smell it, squeeze the blossom end, put the melon down, and repeat. Danika stood frozen across the market, watching her mother do this to eleven melons before her mother was satisfied with her choice and moved on to selecting avocados. For fifteen minutes, Danika observed her mother but never approached her. Never said hello or made small-talk. Never ran over to give her mother a hug. The distance had always been safer, more preferable for both of them.

When her mother died suddenly of a heart attack, Danika hadn't talked to her in a few months. Her father probably never even would have called her about the funeral services if he wasn't so afraid of what it would look like to their family if their only child didn't show up to her own mother's funeral.

Danika walked over to the trash can and fished out the crumpled piece of paper. She smoothed it out on the counter and looked down again at the list. Her eyes scanned down the items: Hike through Tibet. *Ha. Not going to happen.* Learn how to surf in Hawaii. *What was she thinking?* Buy an RV and travel cross country. *Hmm. That does sound like fun.* Take a cooking class. *That's doable.* She knew she was far beyond needing basic cooking lessons, but the thought of taking a cooking class with her favorite chef — an actual Iron Chef — well that was something totally different. She stopped reading. She felt the beginning of something approaching excitement. Danika flipped open the laptop on the counter and typed in a simple search, "The Riverside Café Piermont cooking class" just as the phone rang.

CHAPTER THREE

Sleep rarely eluded Danika. Even in the most stressful situations, she usually fell asleep within minutes of her head hitting the pillow. She powered down when she needed to. But on this night, she lay wide awake in her childhood bedroom. Even though the house was officially hers, and she could sleep wherever she wished, she wasn't able bring herself to sleep in any other room but this one. The only change she'd made upon returning to live in this house was to replace the twin bed with her full-sized bed from the home she once shared with Angela. The bed took up almost all of the space in the tiny room, but that didn't matter. It was the only thing she brought with her. The rest of their furniture and personal items sat collecting dust in a storage locker after she sold their house. Thinking about all that stuff in addition to all the crap here overwhelmed her.

On this night, she lay in bed with the windows open. A light breeze ruffled the yellowed, sheer curtains, and she heard the peeper frogs, occasionally punctuated by a bullfrog, singing away in the creek at the edge of the property. She always loved that sound. Suddenly a ribbon-thin memory floated into her consciousness of a time when she was much younger, before everything got so complicated.

Danika felt different, and it had absolutely nothing to do with a breast cancer prognosis, thank God. The doctor had called right after Natalie left to let her know she was all clear. While she did feel relieved, she didn't exactly feel energized. Instead, she had the vague sensation of wanting to change, of wanting to do more, be more, and get all the misshapen pieces of her broken life back into some semblance of order. That, in itself, was a significant shift. Something had begun to move within her, a sense of self or of truth that had been buried for so long. Like a muscle that goes unused for a long time but is suddenly called upon, the result is soreness and swelling, and mostly discomfort. Danika was definitely in the soreness stage.

There in the dark of her childhood room, as the bullfrogs sang, Danika ultimately decided to sell her parents' house and most everything in it. There wasn't one single thing she wanted to keep except the photo books and keepsakes from her childhood that her mother had stored away in Rubbermaid boxes in the basement. Everything else needed to go. She felt no emotional attachment to any of it. The house and all the musty stuff in it weighed her down, and she was tired of it all. The process of ripping away all the clutter and bottled-up energy made her feel as if she was peeling a giant scab off her very soul. It didn't feel right, but Danika believed she had to do it to survive.

She decided to call Natalie's wife, Suzie, in the morning to talk about listing the house and get a recommendation for someone to organize and manage an estate sale that would include the stuff she had put in storage from her old home with Angela. All of this felt right to her, but she was worried about where she would live next.

Danika lived her whole life in and around Nyack, New York, twenty miles or so north of Manhattan along the Hudson River.

After her father kicked her out of the house, she didn't go far even though she could have. Instead, the better part of her adult life had been spent living in the next little town over called Piermont. She loved the sleepy waterfront village near New York City, dotted with marinas, art galleries, and great restaurants, that possessed an open-minded, almost hippie vibe. Her favorite time of day was sunrise over the Hudson River as it arched above the Tappan Zee Bridge across the river. Although her parents lived only a few miles away, she rarely saw them, usually preferring to steer clear of them altogether. Plus, it wasn't as though they traveled in the same social circles.

Although the house needed cosmetic renovations, it would fetch good money. The bones of the double-ranch house were good, but it was the land it sat on that made the house valuable. Her parents had built the house fifty years ago. They'd moved in when Danika was five years-old, although she only remembered living in that house. She recently uncovered the land deed and was shocked to learn her parents paid only forty thousand dollars for the double lot. Danika expected the house to sell for seven hundred thousand dollars or more. That, in combination with the money she made on the sale of her home with Angela, plus the postal pension, meant she'd live comfortably for the rest of her life. She was still slightly surprised that her father's will granted everything to her. She'd held a suspicion for years that her parents would opt to bequeath their estate to the local church or senior center. But, they didn't. Everything they had went to her.

All of this brought her back to the same question: Where did she want to live? Danika didn't want to pick up and move to Portland, Oregon or Tempe, Arizona. Hell, she didn't even run that far when she was young and had the chance, and it wasn't in her nature to do that now. She had no stomach for starting over like that. The more Danika thought about it, the more an RV appealed to her. No property taxes, and the ability to move wherever she felt like going. While she loved the change in seasons, she'd grown to hate the bitter cold, darkness, and the snow of a New York winter, so the idea of moving someplace warmer from January through April was more than a little appealing to her.

Owning an RV had been in the back of her mind for years. On those random, boring nights when she felt like daydreaming a little, Danika searched for RVs, read reviews, and educated herself to the details of RV ownership. She'd attended the annual RV show at the Javits Center in Manhattan for years, walking in and out of every kind of RV imaginable from forty-six-foot monsters to little travel trailers, and everything in between. Something about living in a mobile home fascinated her because she'd always been so fixed in place. But she still had many steps to take before she'd be ready for this kind of leap. If there was one thing she was good at, it was taking baby steps, or no steps at all.

Her mind wandered from the RV to the cooking class. She'd never taken a course like that in her life, and as a general rule, formal education intimidated her. She never attended college for a four-year degree, and although she got through high school, she didn't exactly excel there either. Danika was always better working with her hands; she was comfortable in constant motion. That's why carrying mail worked for her. She didn't sit in an office all day, forced to deal with inane workplace politics as she stared at a computer screen. Carrying mail wasn't sexy, but, and as much as Danika hated to admit it, she already missed it.

Taking a three-month cooking course at a local Italian restaurant with an Iron Chef was more than scary, with a dash of excitement. The information page clearly stated that class was designed for beginners, and she'd frequented that restaurant enough over the years to have memorized every item on the menu. It wasn't far from home. If she became too uncomfortable, she'd simply take off. The cooking itself didn't scare her. She knew she was an excellent cook. Instead, the social aspect of the class was more concerning. Even after all these years, Danika still felt like she stuck out like a sore thumb whenever she was in a room filled with straight people. It was almost as if she felt like she wore a red flashing neon sign over her forehead that read "Lesbian."

Danika thought about asking Natalie to take the class with her. She knew Natalie would do it for her, but she also felt like she'd be using Natalie as a crutch. If she did this, she'd do it alone.

Frustrated that her brain wouldn't shut off, Danika sighed and decided to get up. It was no use lying in bed cycling through all of these thoughts. She hated insomnia. She rose from the bed and walked across the old pile carpet into the hallway bathroom. She flipped on the light. God, she hated this bathroom. The stall shower/tub combination was the exact color of baby puke, along with the identically colored tile along the walls and floor. Danika looked at herself in the mirror. The harsh lights over the mirrored vanity didn't soften what she saw reflecting back at all, although the green/brown color surrounding her wasn't exactly a flattering tone for any human outside of a morgue.

Danika stared hard at herself in the mirror, looking at herself as if sizing up a stranger. Her square-shaped face looked puffy and washed out, pushing the dark circles around her eyes forward. Her eyebrows needed trimming, plucking, and overall pruning like the yard did. The light brown eyes with flecks of yellow staring back at her seemed flat, tired, and without much spark at all. The crow's feet and wrinkles on her forehead and around her eyes, made her look mid-sixties. Even her light brown hair, more than tinged with gray, lacked luster of any kind. She wasn't able to recall the last time she had a haircut, or even did more than throw it up in a ponytail after a rushed shower. The vague resemblance to Cher in *Moonstruck* before her makeover floated across her mind.

She leaned over the sink further toward the vanity and

turned her head from one side to the other. How on earth did her Roman nose get more prominent than it already was? Apparently, the nose and ears did indeed continue to grow throughout one's life. How awful. Danika made the mistake of lifting up her tee shirt. Why not get a good look at exactly what she had become? The term "glutton for punishment" was accurate in more ways than one. Her once tall and lithe frame looked altogether rounded and soft. She noticed how much she was slouching over the sink and immediately pulled back her shoulders. That was better. Now at least her boobs weren't resting on her belly button. The soufflé she'd chowed down, plus all the other snacks and fast food over the last few months, had taken its toll. She definitely gained weight and needed to do something about it. Danika wasn't fooling herself into thinking she'd fit into her skinny jeans. Those skinny jeans would barely fit over her big toe. Lord knows the time had come and gone for that, but something had to be done. She didn't want to look like this old, sad sack. Danika dropped the front of her Melissa Etheridge concert tee shirt and smoothed it into place.

Jesus, she was a mess. If someone saw her right now, she'd be mistaken for a homeless person. A wafer-thin thought skittered across her mind: *Self-care is sexy.* The mere thought of the word "sexy" made a wry laugh spring up from her throat, although it sounded more like an outright cough. She hadn't felt sexy in a very long time. Forget months. Years. Many years. And with the overall look she had going on, it was as if she tattooed "I'm never having sex again" on her forehead, which at her age, was more than a real possibility.

Danika walked downstairs to the kitchen trying to think of the last time she had sex. Not being able to remember it was a bad sign. She tried to pinpoint the moment when she gave up wanting to have sex, be touched, satiated.

One night before Angela got sick, they'd gone out to dinner to celebrate their sixteenth anniversary while they were visiting Provincetown. The restaurant called Ceraldi's located in quaint Wellfleet, named for the chef, Michael Ceraldi, was a small space that only offered a seven-course prix-fixe tasting menu sourced from seasonal, hyper-local ingredients. Ceraldi's wanted to treat diners to a unique culinary experience in time and place. During their excellent first course of a single Wellfleet oyster harvested only hours before dinner service, Danika had looked up at Angela. In her mind, she remembered thinking that oysters were known to be aphrodisiacs, but she and Angela would need dozens of them to spark anything that resembled passion between them. Angela looked tired. No longer did Danika feel the pitter-patter of butterflies in her stomach, and that was a shame. She tried like hell that night to find some shred of commonality between them aside from the house to talk about, but each time she came up empty, creating caverns in their dinner conversations that were miles deep.

After dinner, they returned to their colorful room at Roux Bed and Breakfast where the relaxing scent of lavender essential oil infused the room and the bed linens. By the time Danika had opened the bathroom door after a quick shower, Angela had fallen asleep in the middle of the bed, spread-eagled with her red pajamas adding more color to the already bright room.

Their relationship had deteriorated to such a degree that it felt more like a roommate situation than a partnership. By the time Angela came home from the doctor after a routine mammo-gram and visit to the gynecologist on that horrible day two years ago, Danika had already been working up the courage to break up with her. She paced around the house for hours before Angela had returned home, trying to memorize the exact right words to say to keep the wounding and pain to a minimum.

As tricky as leaving Angela would have been, at the time, Danika felt ready to start over and begin the process of disengaging her life from Angela's, before it was too late to meet anyone new. But, everything changed when Angela came home from the doctor looking like she'd been crying for hours, telling Danika they had to talk. They'd sat down at the kitchen counter. Danika made her a cup of chamomile tea while Angela alternated sobbing and staring off into space. Angela's hands shook so hard the tea splashed out of the mug. Angela said the words in a halting, broken tone like Morse code over the sea and sky: phrases like "breast cancer" and "stage four" and "it's in the lymph nodes" and "five percent probability of survival." Danika hung onto the edges of the countertop like she was in a ship listing heavily to one side, knowing it would inevitably sink with her in it.

Looking back, Danika knew she made the right decision to stay with Angela through the stage four breast-cancer diagnosis, and the horrible chemo and radiation treatments. Although she was no longer in love with Angela, she did love her. They were best friends, and friends didn't run away during times like those. No, she would stick it out.

Staying by her side during the short six months that Angela bravely battled cancer never felt like the wrong choice, but it often felt unbearable. As Angela's health deteriorated, it became customary for Danika to meet Natalie at the Chips Pub for a beer or a bourbon in the evening to decompress. One night, Danika sat in the corner stool of the bar and downed a double of Jack Daniels Honey and had no words. She had nothing in the tank. Natalie sat with her on those nights, and many others, letting Danika take a breath, rant and rave, cry or do whatever she had to do to deal with the pain of watching Angela waste away in front of her very eyes.

When Angela's time came, Danika sat beside her, holding her hand as Angela took her last breath. The room had been so quiet as Angela took quick, shallow breaths, her eyes wild with fear. At the nearby nurses' station, a group of doctors and nurses sang happy birthday as Danika tried to console Angela. "You can let go, Ang. Let go. It's alright. It's time, and you've been so brave. Soon you won't feel any more pain," she'd cooed in Angela's ear, trying so hard to make the wildness in Angela's eyes disappear. And then, it was over. Just like that. No crescendo of music, no particular moment where they made eye contact or squeezed one another's hands. One moment Angela was there, the next she was gone.

Danika remembered walking past the nurses' station afterward, seeing a mess of a half-eaten cake on the countertop. That, in combination with the antiseptic hospital smell and the reminder that Angela would never celebrate another birthday, sent Danika running for the bathroom where she heaved up what was left of the stale hospital sandwich she'd eaten several hours before.

What she had not expected was to go from that emotional roller coaster directly into becoming the primary caretaker for her dying father. What little life force remained in Danika after Angela's death was unceremoniously sucked out of her by her him. But, here she was, a survivor in her own right, too. Natalie had been right—it was time for Danika to finally start taking care of herself again. The trouble was, she was so out of practice it all felt foreign to her as if she'd stepped off an airplane into a foreign country.

Danika made herself a pot of coffee. There was no way she would get any sleep tonight. She made a mental note to schedule a hair appointment, pronto. She also decided that she had to get out of this house. She loved being a homebody, but she'd taken that concept to a whole new level lately. It was time to get back to the land of the living.

CHAPTER FOUR

A week later, Danika sat outside the local coffee shop overlooking the Hudson River, reading the first few pages of *The Seat of the Soul* by Gary Zukav. Typically, these types of self help, spirituality books didn't appeal to her, but it caught her attention on the shelf. Danika was, after all, drinking a cappuccino in the middle of the afternoon alone. She looked up from her book at the sunlight dancing on the water and chuckled to herself. The mere act of sitting outside in the middle of the day, alone, drinking cappuccino, and reading, seemed so far flung from her usual routine it was almost laughable. She felt slightly ridiculous, as though her very presence stuck out like a sore thumb causing strangers to stop and stare.

As she sipped her cappuccino, savoring the rich, warm, and almost comforting fragrance of it, a voice from behind Danika startled her. "Danika Russo? Is that you?"

She placed her mug down on the metal table and turned over her shoulder. "Yes?"

"I thought that was you. I'm so sorry to hear about your

father." A well-dressed senior woman stood over the bistro table smiling down at Danika.

It took a moment for Danika to place her. "Yes, hello, Mrs. Stevens. Thank you." Danika looked up, immediately self-conscious.

"My, you look wonderful. Have you done something different with your hair?"

Danika self-consciously touched her shoulder-length brown locks. "Yes, actually, I spent a fortune at the salon getting a cut and color."

"Well, it looks great. If I didn't know better, I'd think you were in your thirties." Mrs. Stevens winked conspiratorially at Danika.

Danika laughed. "Ahh, my thirties, now those were good years. Please say hello to Mr. Stevens for me."

"I will, dear. Take care." The old woman tottered off as Danika leaned back in her bistro chair. She smiled. Even though Mrs. Stevens, who'd been a longtime friend of her mother's, was probably in her eighties and half-blind, the idea that she noticed Danika's appearance perked Danika up considerably. *A compliment is a compliment*, she thought to herself. Danika re-opened her book and began to read.

An excerpt from the book that resonated deep inside her talked about our higher purpose, and aligning our thoughts, emotions, and actions to helps us live with purpose and meaning. Re-reading the excerpt five or six times, she wondered what the highest part of herself was. It had never even occurred to her to think about possessing a higher self or calling. She grew up the only child of Barb and Frank Russo in Nyack, New York. She'd never excelled at anything. She delivered mail. Never had children. She puttered in the garden and loved to cook. She never actually expected much from her life beyond the mundane. This book was causing her to look at herself differently, as if her own thoughts were somehow responsible for her life, and by changing her dreams, she was in control of changing her life. Maybe for some, the idea would be clear as day, but for her, it was revolutionary. And it caused her to look around at herself and the way she stood in the world with a different view as if each detail of the sun or the sky, her hand resting on the page of the book, all of it served a specific purpose at that moment.

Danika wondered about her purpose. She thought back to her childhood and adolescence. Danika never possessed a strong sense of what to be; never felt a driving purpose or need to be anything special. In fact, she'd spent the better part of her life knowing she wasn't exceptional at all. Understanding her sexuality and overcoming the Catholic guilt she was raised with had forced her into doing the opposite of wanting to stand out or be unique—it had subconsciously trained her into only wanting to blend in and pass by unnoticed. Now, here she was, a fifty-five-year-old woman sitting at an outdoor coffee shop having her first official crisis of conscience. Her mind shifted to an image of a horse on a race track with blinders on. For some inexplicable reason, she decided to remove the blinders over her own eyes, and the result was a woman in her mid-fifties blinking like she'd never seen—really seen—anything before.

Danika felt a hand on her shoulder. She jumped with a start, dropping the book onto the sidewalk.

"Woah, relax. It's only me!" Natalie bent down and picked up the book. She glanced at the title, then to Danika. Her eyes widened. "Wait. Let me get this straight. You're sitting outside in the middle of the day..." Natalie leaned forward and peeked into Danika's coffee mug before continuing. "And you're drinking cappuccino. I never even knew you liked cappuccino. And you're reading *The Seat of the Soul*, and you had your hair done. Eyebrows too, from the looks of it. Who are you and what have

you done with my best friend?" Natalie plopped down in the
bistro chair next to Danika, openly staring at her.

"Oh, shut up. Apparently, I do like cappuccino, something I
did not know until today."

"And the book?"

Danika huffed. "What? I do read, Natalie."

"Of course, you read, but books about the soul?"

"I don't know. It appealed to me. I don't know why." Danika
paused. "Do you know what your purpose is?"

"You mean like in life?" Natalie asked, looking quizzically at
her friend.

"Yeah."

Natalie sat back in her chair. A waitress popped by the table.
"I'll have what she had," she said to the woman before continuing. "Way to launch right into the heavy stuff. Whatever
happened to 'Hey Natalie, what's shakin'?'"

Danika eyed Natalie with a raised eyebrow.

"Okay, okay. I know that look. Jesus. Let me at least get situ-
ated before we contemplate the meaning of life." Natalie leaned
back, crossed her legs, and looked out at the Hudson River. She
took a breath. "If I had to think about it, I'd say to be a parent. I
think I was put on this earth to parent Lexi and David, and to
love Suzie."

Danika nodded. She expected her friend to say that. It made
sense. Natalie was born to parent and took to it immediately.

"Why all the self-reflection?" Natalie asked.

"This book got me thinking is all. I've been sitting here trying
to figure out what my purpose is. I don't think, no wait, I know for
a fact that I never gave it a thought before now."

The waitress delivered the cappuccino. "That's great. I mean
it's great you're thinking like this," said Natalie.

"No, it's not. Nat, I'm fifty-five years old. It's a little late to be
thinking about my purpose, don't you think?" Danika looked out

over the water, trying to settle the anger she felt rising inside her like an oncoming tide. She stuffed it aside and took a sip of her cappuccino.

"Don't start with the 'I'm too old to think, or do, or become' bullshit. You are where you are."

"That's profound," Danika remarked flatly.

"Well, it's true. Dr. Seuss said, 'sometimes the questions are complicated, and the answers are simple.'"

"What are you telling me that my purpose is staring at me in the face and I don't see it, a la Dr. Seuss?"

"No, not exactly." Natalie sipped her cappuccino and left a froth mustache in place for good measure, which in turn made Danika laugh. She winked and wiped it, then continued, "I get that you're questioning things. Doing that is good. The past is the past. There's no sense in getting stuck into thinking you should have had this all figured out years ago. You are where you are in your life, and maybe you were meant to open up to the possibilities of life at this stage in it. That's all I'm saying."

Danika hesitated. "You mean it's not too late for me to figure out my purpose?"

"Of course not. Because you're in your fifties doesn't mean you have to stop wanting things from life. It doesn't mean you should stop growing or changing or becoming who you were meant to be."

"How do you always know what to say to me?" Danika asked as she squeezed her friend's hand from across the small bistro table.

"Woman, I've known you so long that sometimes I think I get you more than I get me. You've struggled for years. Maybe now is the time for you to step outside yourself and work at it. After all, the new hair, and this look, is a step in the right direction. If you keep this up, Suzie will wonder whether that first kiss when we were eighteen meant anything."

"Funny you should mention that kiss, I thought about it the other night," Danika mused.

Natalie leaned in, batting her eyelashes for good measure. "You were? And did it get you all hot and bothered?"

"Knock it off. That's gross. You're like my sister. No, I wasn't thinking about the kiss in that way, I thought about the aftermath with my parents, and how horrible that all was."

Natalie leaned back in her chair sucking in her breath. "Woo, yeah, that part sucked. It was awful." She crossed her arms. "I sweat thinking about it. Thank God that's over and done with."

"You can say that again," Danika agreed.

"Oh, before I forget, Suzie told me the guy is coming tomorrow morning to install the sign in front of your house. She also told me everything is all set, that the house will list tomorrow morning officially." Natalie took a sip of her cappuccino. "You excited?"

"Definitely. I can't wait to sell that place."

"So, what's next?"

"What are you doing this afternoon?" Danika asked.

"Nothing. I'm all yours, babe. What are we doing?"

"I got an appointment to look at RVs," Danika replied.

"Hey, that sounds awesome." Natalie polished off her cappuccino. "I'm in, but only if you take me someplace great for dinner. Suzie has a broker's open house party tonight, and lord knows I don't want to be around a bunch of real estate agents. They talk entirely too much. Like sitting in a room with a bunch of cheerleaders."

"You've got a deal. Let's get going." Danika placed some cash on the table and slipped her book into her bag. She felt excited about the future for the first time in a long time. *It must be the haircut*, she mused. The idea of looking at somewhere new to live made Danika nervous and excited at the same time, but she needed to start somewhere, and this was as good of a place to begin as any.

Three hours later, Danika sat in the driver's seat of her Jeep Cherokee with her hands on the steering wheel, staring out into the parking lot as the car idled. Natalie sat beside her in the passenger seat. Neither spoke. After about twenty seconds, Natalie shouted, "Woo-hoo!! Oh, my God, I can't *believe* you bought an RV! Holy crap!" Natalie slapped Danika on the shoulder knocking her out of her stunned silence.

"I bought an RV," Danika said simply, as if she was trying to convince herself of the same fact. "I bought an RV!!" she said again, this time louder and more insistent. "I can't believe I freaking bought it!"

"You walked into that place like John Wayne. I'm telling you I've never seen you like that in my life. You sauntered in like 'Hey partner, you see that RV over there? You're going to sell that RV to me today for the price I want.' You pointed to the one you wanted, and that was it. I'm telling you, I've never been so stunned and turned on at the same time in all my life."

Danika laughed at the characterization. She did walk in like John Wayne knowing she wanted the Cruiser Volante thirty-two-foot, fully loaded fifth-wheel with the hickory interior. She walked into the dealer knowing what added features she had to have, and where she had room to negotiate on price. The poor, wide-eyed junior salesman didn't know what hit him. After it was all said and done, she bargained for a slew of extra features including two LED televisions, a second A/C in the bedroom, rear camera, and more. Danika laughed recalling how Natalie stood there with her mouth hanging open as Danika and the salesman went back and forth.

"Suzie better sell my house fast because I wrote a massive check."

"A huge check," Natalie nodded in assent.

"Well, I guess I better sell my Jeep and buy a new heavy-duty pickup truck to haul that beast," Danika mused.

"You're buying a truck too? I'm literally in lesbian heaven right now. Next, you're going to tell me we have to stop at Home Depot for a few power tools. Seriously, though, I can't do it unless you feed me. Real food. I'm about ready to pass out from exhaustion."

Danika's eyes crinkled as her mouth turned upwards into a huge smile. A full-on belly-laugh took hold of her. She gripped the steering wheel a little tighter and laughed so hard her eyes began to tear up. The infectious mirth carried over to Natalie, who also began laughing. The two of them hooted and cackled, causing the Jeep to shake back and forth. Danika didn't remember the last time she'd laughed hard enough hard to feel it in her toes. It felt incredible. It felt right. It was about damned time.

CHAPTER FIVE

Three weeks later, the sun pounded down from a cloudless sky, scorching just about everything in its path. The relative comfort of June had given way to the unrelenting heat and humidity of July. The grass wilted and the flowers drooped their colorful heads, as if trying to shade their delicate stems from the blistering sunlight. When Danika was a teenager, she loved the summer heat, often jogging during lunch at the hottest point of the day to tan and exercise at once. Now, it was a different story. She detested the stifling weather nearly as much as she hated the sub-zero temperatures of February.

Actually, on days like this, she despised herself for briefly contemplating a slight preference for cold weather over this. At least in the winter, one could bundle up. There were only so many layers one could strip off in ninety-eight-degree weather. She tried fanning herself with a notebook while she rocked to and fro on the front porch swing that had a "sold" ticket hanging from one of the chain loops. Fanning herself did little to give her any relief, so she tossed the notebook aside, tipped her head back against the cushion, propped her bare feet up on the other side of the swing, and closed her eyes. She was sticky and dirty and in dire need of a shower.

The late afternoon cicada song was long and low, a constant low-pitched hum that had an altogether relaxing effect on Danika. A few tasks still needed to be done. Packing, hauling, trashing, but right now, her mind wandered, and the same old rudderless aura took hold. One moment she swatted a fly and cursed the heat. The next, she was ten years old, sitting on the same swing in precisely the same position. It was funny how times passed, she thought: life is lived, then one day we realized we were no longer the children we used to be, but the very same children had been, all at once.

Out of nowhere, the pang in her heart lurched forth. It always hit her at odd moments. Usually, she did her best to ignore it by moving onto something else to focus on. She looked around the deck at all the crap that wasn't hers and would soon be gone, but the empty space in her chest demanded her attention. Danika's heart burned like the heat of the sun for someone to love. She yearned for the touch of someone she'd never even met. She had this certainty that person was out there in the vastness of the unknown, but all the wondering, and most of all, the wishing, exhausted her. The ache of her loneliness bubbled to the surface at random times, and this was one of those times. Truthfully, she was far too exhausted both mentally and physically to have the energy for anyone else, but still, the pull for it remained.

After only three days on the market, her parents' house became caught up in a bidding war. She ultimately sold the house forty-thousand dollars over asking price, for cash, in return for a thirty-day closing. She'd finished a three-day estate sale, thrilled to have nearly all of the junk either sold, donated, or trashed. The interior of the house had mostly been emptied, including the storage locker and garage. She glanced over to her new home, the fifth wheel travel trailer, parked alongside the house in the driveway, connected to a new steel-gray Ford Super Duty pickup truck.

Danika dozed off on the porch swing that now belonged to someone else, adrift and pensive. Would life always be this challenging—and lonely—for the rest of her days? Making friends had never come naturally to her, and she found herself more withdrawn as she aged. The excitement of city life or bustling streets never appealed to her, which left her prospects of meeting anyone new, or anyone to fill this gaping hole inside her heart, more than a little limited. Danika sighed a long and low sigh. The cicadas' rhythmic *cccht, cccht – cccht, cccht* was the only response.

Danika probably would have fallen asleep if it wasn't for the sound of a car pulling up the driveway. As the car door slammed closed, Danika opened one eye and peered down at her watch, which read three forty-five. She mustered up the energy to turn her head as she heard "Hey Danika!"

"Hey, Pete," Danika's voice was tattered and filled with exhaustion. She'd met Pete ten years ago at the Post Office, and they became good friends over the years. Straight, and now married with four little ones, Pete perennially looked like a strapping lumberjack with his reddish beard and rotating wardrobe of plaid shirts. Danika continued, "What's up? I'd offer you a place to sit, but as you can see, I'm in the only seat, and I'm too tired to move. Cold beer is in the cooler." Danika pointed to a blue Igloo cooler on the corner of the deck.

"You look wiped, but wow, everything is almost gone, huh?" Pete peeked inside the front windows into an empty living room before handing a Sam Adams summer ale to Danika and helping himself to one. He slid the cooler closer to the porch swing and sat down on it.

"I'm nearly done," Danika replied as she opened the bottle and took a swig. "Now I need to know where I'm going to park

my new house." Danika hadn't thought this part through carefully enough when she'd made the impulse purchase with
Natalie. She wasn't prepared to drive cross-country, but there
were virtually no RV parks in the area to take a trailer her size.
She'd been on a constant merry-go-round of denial about where
she would go, but had little time or energy to think about it much
over the last few weeks.

"That's why I'm here. You are going to love me after I tell you
this," Pete smiled, showing his perfect teeth.

"I love you already. Did you win the lottery or something?"

"No, I wish. I found the perfect spot for you to move your
trailer."

Danika's eyes widened. She leaned forward in the swing,
causing the rusty chains to squeak in objection. "Where?"

"Not far. Valley Cottage. A buddy I played baseball in
college with named Mike Dunham has a camp. Well, he calls it a
camp. He has a bunch of land with nothing on it. He'd been planning to put in a mobile home but never got around to finishing
before his divorce. He landed a job in Denver and is moving out
there. I told him you had this sweet new RV but nowhere to put
it. He offered up his place." Pete took a long swig of beer, looking
proud as punch.

"Wow, Pete. That's amazing, Valley Cottage is only a few
miles away. But, I need electric, water, and septic. I'm not going
to have anyplace to pump out once we get into the winter."

"Oh yeah, I almost forgot the best part. The electrical, cable,
well, and sewer were already set up for a mobile home. He had a
pad installed that's plenty big enough for the trailer. I'm telling
you; it's perfect. You'll have five acres and a pond all to yourself,
but won't be far from here."

Danika was in shock. There had to be a catch. It sounded too
perfect. "How much does he want for it?" she asked cautiously.

"Honestly, he didn't even say anything about rent. You'll

have to pay your own utilities, and if you wanted to throw him something extra every month, he'd be thrilled. I give him a year before he'll probably sell the land to you anyhow. I can't imagine he'll be coming back once he hits Denver. The guy is a big skier."

Danika sipped her beer and considered all that Pete told her. Usually, she'd hem and haw, analyze and overthink, want to check the place out five times, but a new person was slowly emerging from inside Danika. She jumped up from the porch swing, bent over, and hugged Pete. "I owe you big time. Give me ten minutes to shower and lock this place up. I'm already hitched; I can follow you there!"

"You won't be disappointed, Danika. I promise!" Pete winked.

CHAPTER SIX

Danika waited for Pete to unlock the gate to the property as her pickup truck hummed. She turned the vent; soon, cold air blew on her face. Pete swung the metal gate open across the dirt road. The metal archway over the gate looked custom made, with "The Golden Oak" written in wrought iron. The sign and gate alone hooked Danika. She liked that the gate locked, helping to keep out any trespassers. Pete hopped back in his pickup and continued down the long, straight dirt road. Danika followed slowly behind. The wide-open feel of the property struck her immediately. Most of the available land in this area had long since been gobbled up and sub-divided, making the property even more of a gem. After a quarter-mile or ride past long grasses and wildflowers, Danika saw the concrete pad that was plenty big enough. She swung around, driving the pickup onto the pad, pulling up slowly until the trailer was centered and straight. She set the brake and hopped out of her truck. Pete already stood beside the RV, hands on his hips, smiling broadly.

"Didn't I tell you it was perfect?" Pete beamed.

"You did. And you meant it. I can't believe this, Pete. It's beautiful." Danika walked around towards a low-standing cedar shed set up next to the pad with all the necessary connections to electric, cable, septic, and seemingly already prepped for winter with a new space heater. All the lines looked unused. She tented her hand and looked out toward another much larger cedar shed about twenty feet away. "What's in there?" Danika asked.

"Dunno. Let's go check it out." Pete and Danika walked over to the shed that had at least a half-cord of firewood neatly stacked up beside it. Danika noted the large chopping block next to it. Pete saw the padlock and tried the same key he'd used for the front gate. "Bingo," he said as the lock clicked open. He slid the door open to peek in. A wall of hot air slammed into them. A small, well-organized workshop, with tools neatly hanging from hooks on the pegboard wall, took up the left side of the shed. In the center sat an old cast iron wood stove with dry wood and kindling already neatly stacked nearby. The right side of the shed stored a John Deere ride-on lawnmower, other lawn and garden equipment, outdoor furniture, and what looked like a screened in pop-up tent.

"Wow." Danika breathed. They stepped out of the shed and walked southwest toward a huge pond. They passed a brand new, but empty, chicken coop. A large circular area with white pea-stone and a custom-built fire pit had been built in front of the pond because of the expansive views. Two wood posts with large hooks dangling off the front of each stood to the left under a huge maple tree that Danika quickly surmised had been installed for a hammock. She looked out over the pond toward the swim platform in the middle as the hazy late-afternoon sun left an orange glow over the water. The large oak trees around the pond shuffled their leaves ever-so-slightly as if to welcome Danika. "Pete, am I dreaming?" Danika whispered.

"I know, right? It kind of feels like that. It's like this place was made for you or something."

"If you told me to imagine the perfect place to live, I couldn't have imagined this." Tears ran down Danika's cheeks. The utter serenity of the place took her breath away. At that moment, Danika realized how uncomfortable she'd been living with Angela, then with her father in her childhood home. None of those places ever felt like her. That was it. Discomfort. She had merely subsisted in those houses, under trying circumstances, for so long that she forgot how to live. Now that she was in this place of ample open space, she felt able to breathe, and it felt remarkable.

Pete sensed Danika's emotions and wrapped his arm protectively around her shoulders. He didn't try to talk or tell her to stop crying. He stood with his arm around her giving her the space to let it all go. And let it all go she did. After a few minutes of crying, Danika wiped her tears away. "You'd never know you grew up in a household of all women," Danika said, chuckling.

"You betcha. I learned to keep my mouth shut and let a woman cry it out. Plus, I kind of figured those weren't tears of sorrow. I know you're relieved to be out of that house," Pete commented.

Danika responded by tipping her head against Pete's shoulder.

"What do you say we get you set up?"

"I can handle it from here, Pete." Danika checked her watch. "You have four little ones at home, and it's bath time. Monica could probably use a break by now."

"Okay. I'll swing by after work tomorrow and check on you," said Pete. He tossed Danika the key to the gate and shed. She caught it and waved at Pete. "I owe you big time," she declared.

"Damn right you do. Free beer for life," Pete yelled as he climbed into his pickup and revved the engine.

After Pete drove off and the dust of the dirt road settled,

Danika got to work setting up her new home. It wasn't long before she had to break out the bug spray. Man, the mosquitoes were huge. She made a mental note to set up the pop-up screened-in-tent she saw in the shed in the morning. Danika made another mental note to buy a snow plow for the pickup truck before autumn. The prices would be lower now, and she'd most definitely need a plow to get down that long driveway.

Setting up the electrical lines, cable, water, gray, and black lines, took much longer than she expected because it was the first time she was doing it, and the learning curve was steep, not to mention she'd already put in a full day at her parents' house with very little food. It was long past nine o'clock by the time she finished. She stepped away from the RV and looked at her work. She deployed the awning with LED lights, and double-checked that she'd connected all the lines correctly. Everything seemed to be working well.

A few minutes later, she stepped into her new home that smelled new, and was immediately thankful she'd splurged on the luxury trailer graded for four-season use. It was as if she knew all along she'd end up right here in this spot. She said a silent thank-you for the high-capacity air-conditioning system as she felt the fresh air pouring forth. She walked over to the kitchen sink, testing the faucet. Sure enough, both hot and cold water worked fine. On a lark, she flipped on the television and was shocked to see a picture appear on the screen. Even the cable worked. She powered up the cable modem she found boxed in the shed, and saw the internet button light up. How about that? She flipped off the television but connected her cell phone to the Bluetooth speakers. Within a matter of minutes, she'd synched to her iTunes library, listening to her "Long Night Chill" playlist that started with Corinne Bailey Rae's "Put Your Records On."

Danika stripped off her sweaty clothes and stepped into her new shower on the first official night in her new home. As she let the cold water beat down over her head matting her hair down, she began to dance naked in the shower. Danika Russo shimmied naked, singing out loud. Who was she and what had she done with her old self? The old Danika would have scoffed at herself singing and shaking around the shower, but this new person decided that was rubbish. If she wanted to sing out loud in her own shower, she would damned well do it with a shake, shake, shake.

Danika was home. Now if she could only find someone with whom to share her life. She washed her hair and scrubbed the grime and dirt of the day off her body. After she dried herself off, she stood looking at her reflection in the mirror. Already, she looked better than she had that night two months ago when she looked at herself this way in her parents' house. Maybe the light was kinder, or maybe she did look better. All the activity and stress of the past two months helped shave off some extra weight. After applying moisturizing lotion and brushing her teeth, she walked into her bedroom. The ridiculousness of having a king-size bed all to herself made her laugh. After laying a towel down over the pillow for her wet hair, Danika tossed her sleep shirt aside, uncharacteristically deciding that tonight, she would sleep naked. She turned off the music from her cell phone and put the phone in silence-mode next to her bed.

After scooting over to the center of the mattress, Danika stretched out her arms and legs as if she was making snow angels in bed. She giggled like a little girl, then leaned over, and slid open the small window on one side of the bed. She heard the peeper frogs and bullfrogs from the pond and immediately felt her shoulders drop an inch as her body relaxed into the new mattress. Danika began her new nightly gratitude ritual and mentally thought about all the things to be grateful for. Pete came first on her list for finding her this magical place. Before she could think of anything—or anyone else—Danika fell fast asleep.

CHAPTER SEVEN

A buzz hearkened off in the distance. A vibration. Buzz. Buzz. Buzz. Danika dreamed of a giant bumblebee flying over a pond as the sun rose. *Wait one second,* she thought, as she gained consciousness. *That's not a bumblebee. That's your cell phone.* Danika peeled her eyes open. She lay in the middle of the bed in virtually the same position she fell asleep. She rolled onto her side and grabbed the cell phone. "Hello?" she croaked out in a pre-coffee, not-in-a-sexy-way morning tone.

"Hello, is this Danika Russo?" a friendly voice on the other end of the line asked.

"Yes. That's me." Was it the IRS? The police? Publishers Clearing House?

"Miss Russo, this is André from the Riverside Café. I'm calling to remind you of our first cooking class tonight with Chef Antonio Servante."

Danika sat upright in bed. *Shit. The cooking class.* She totally forgot.

"Oh yes, that's right. Tonight. I'll be there," Danika stammered.

"Wonderful. We'll see you tonight at five o'clock," André replied.

"Okay. Thanks for calling." Danika said as she ended the call and flopped back down on the bed, suddenly self-consciousness of her nakedness. *Jesus, how early did that guy have to call?* Danika thought, moderately annoyed. She looked at the phone and was shocked to see it was ten-thirty in the morning. Ten-thirty. She hadn't slept this good in twenty years. She stretched her arms over her head and extended her legs and toes as far as they'd go. With much to do today, she wouldn't let her nerves center on the cooking class.

Danika popped out of bed and scooped her light brown hair up in a ponytail. She threw on a pair of baggy cargo shorts and a sports bra and rummaged around her still disorganized dresser drawers and closet for a tank top and baseball cap. Then, she headed to the kitchen for a quick cup of coffee and cereal. Breakfast of champions.

One of the highlights about the RV was the large picture window in the central living area. And on this lot, with the views and open space all around, it made the inside seem doubly spacious and bright. She leaned up against the center island looking out at the pond as she drank a steaming cup of fragrant Italian hazelnut dark-roast coffee in the mid-morning, summertime quiet. The coffee tasted great because all the relief and joy of her new surroundings were wrapped up inside the mug and in every sip. Happiness. There it was again bubbling up curving her lips into a smile.

A few minutes later, she was hit with a wall of heat as she exited the RV that she tried her best to ignore. Her first order of business was to set up the outdoor furniture around the fire pit and get that screened-in tent set up before the giant mosquitoes attacked again. The furniture turned out to be easy enough, and she even found a new hammock in a bag that she quickly dispatched between the two poles by the pond. The ten-by-ten tent proved to be tricky. With no instructions and little familiarity with the product, she struggled for the better part of an hour to get the blasted thing set up. She glared at the label "Made in China" and determined to find out if the Chinese intentionally created products with forty-two parts and one line of terribly translated instructions to torture Americans. Her annoyance waned once she sat at the picnic table inside the bug-free tent drinking ice water.

Next, she set up a small outdoor propane grill and the outdoor shower that was attached to the RV. Both would prove useful. Then, she hopped on the John Deere to cut down the tall grass around the RV and pond for a nicely manicured lawn. It would keep the ticks away, plus she loved the smell of fresh cut grass. It took several passes to cut up the tall, thick grass but it smelled so amazingly crisp and summery that she didn't mind the oncoming sunburn on her shoulders, neck, and arms. As she mowed, her mind wandered away from all the thoughts of things she had to do and settled on absolutely nothing except turning to the left, watching out for rocks, following her line in the grass. There were no guarantees beyond this present moment. She merely had to be herself. No more, no less. She listened to the birds and the breeze through the leaves on the trees, and she felt content, free, as if all the past struggles of her life formed a patchwork quilt that held meaning, but no longer defined her.

After she returned the mower to the shed, she walked to the edge of the pond and looked around. Convinced she was alone, she took off her sweaty tank top and cargo shorts and walked into the pond wearing only her sports bra and tomboy underwear. She expected her feet to squish into the mud, but Pete's friend Mike Dunham had thought of everything. The pea stone extended to form a sort of runway into the water. Warm water covered her feet in the shallower water, but as she moved out into deeper water, it became refreshingly cool. Broad and deep, with clear water and little algae, the picturesque pond anchored the property and everything on it. If a piece of land could be its own universe, the circular body of water was the sun that everything else revolved around.

Danika swam out to the swim platform and climbed up. On her back with a forearm shielding the sun from her eyes, she felt the light rock and tip of the swim dock. It was intoxicatingly relaxing. As she lay there, a fleeting band of self-consciousness flowed through her. She was, after all, wearing only a sports bra and briefs, and her body wasn't exactly firm and toned in all the right places. But she let the feeling of self-doubt pass through her. There was no reason for it, and it served no purpose. She was who she was, and that meant she wasn't perfect in a variety of ways. She felt the needle pricks of the sharp sun drying the water from her body. It occurred to her that she hadn't really felt anything with her body in such a long time. No one had touched her in years. She ran her hand down the side of her face, down her right breast, her belly to her crotch and let her hand rest there for a few moments. When was the last time she'd touched herself? Masturbation had never been her thing. She didn't actually do it for the first time until she was in her thirties. It's not that she was a prude or anything, she simply had never given self-pleasure much thought. Here in this new home, it was as if her body was waking up from a long hibernation. An awareness grew within her like a small seedling. She slid her hand underneath her underwear, touching herself. She felt the weight of her own hand on her crotch and shifted slightly. Her hips began to slowly rock against her hand. Her breath quickened. Danika closed her eyes and felt water rolling off her shoulders onto the dock. A rolling tide of pent-up energy flowed from her center out her limbs and top of her head. Wave after wave rolled through her, over her, from somewhere deep inside her as the sun warmed her skin, transferring some unseen energy to her beating heart.

Danika took a deep breath and inhaled the verdant dried grasses, a ribbon of honeysuckle floated across her face as the breeze shifted the air, rustling the darkening green mid-summer leaves. It was all a symphony, and it played for her. Apparently, this was what contentment felt like. She had never really known the sensation before. Not like this. Not ever to this degree. If she was to spend the rest of her life alone, she'd be able to do it here.

Danika dozed and lounged for the remainder of the afternoon in the hammock under the huge maple tree until hunger pangs and a keen sense of urgency to be on time for her cooking class took hold. She showered and decided to wear a pair of khaki shorts and a dark red V-neck tee shirt. She thought about leaving her hair down but decided it was a cooking class, not a date, so she pulled it back into a low ponytail. She even applied dark brown eyeliner to her upper lids, making her speckled brown eyes look even more luminous than they already were. She stared at her appearance in the mirror. *Pretty good*, she thought.

It was now or never. Danika had opened many new doors over these last few weeks, making her more willing to explore and try something new than she ever had in the past. Before overthinking her choice, she grabbed her wallet and keys and headed for the door.

CHAPTER EIGHT

Twenty minutes later, Danika sat inside the cab of her pickup truck worried sick about going inside the Riverside Café. She observed a few people, mostly women, enter. She looked down at her watch. It was nearly time. She needed to stop acting like a stick in the mud, as her grandmother used to say. She hopped down from the pickup and quickly walked inside.

First, she was hit with the cold blast of air conditioning. Then she heard a boisterous "Ciao, bella! Welcome. May I get your name?"

"Hi. I'm Danika. Danika Russo."

"Yes, Ms. Russo. Thank you. Please. Take an apron and go right into the kitchen. The class will begin momentarily. We are waiting for one other person."

"Okay. Thanks," replied Danika. Too late to bolt. She took a crisp white apron off the pile and put it on, tying it loosely around her thick waist. She pushed the double doors of the kitchen open immediately struck by the brightness as compared to the relative duskiness of the dining room. She'd never been in a commercial kitchen before. Huge, with long stainless steel open-base workta-bles, several gas ranges, double door ovens, fryers, steamers, commercial broilers, and what looked to Danika like an entire table full of immersion circulators filled the space. Her obsession with the Food Network presented her with a working knowledge of most of the equipment. Her overall impression suggested an immaculate and well-organized kitchen.

Danika took her place on the far end of a long stainless-steel counter along with four women—two were older, and two were definitely younger. There were two young couples at another table in front of her, where both of the bearded, manicured, man-bunned men tried to look hip and cool about being there. *Defi-nitely, newlyweds* thought Danika to herself as she watched the two couples interact. She tended to size up a room to determine if there were any other people like her in it. From the looks of it, they were all straight, making her feel uncomfortable.

Before she became too caught up in feeling out of place, the chef entered the kitchen. She recognized him immediately because she'd seen him on the Food Network's Iron Chef Gaunt-let. Tall and lean with a well-trimmed Anderson Cooper-ish haircut and salt and pepper stubble, he began, "Hello everyone! Welcome to the Riverside Café. I'm Chef Antonio Servante."

The kitchen doors swung open. Everyone paused to look, including Danika, who turned her head slowly to the left. A woman entered the room, her large light brown topaz eyes meeting Danika's at precisely the same moment. She stood in the doorway as if her mere presence held up the very building itself. She was taller than average, and Danika felt sure the woman was stable, steady, like someone who'd stand unbending in the middle of a raging river with her feet firmly planted on the ground.

She wore faded jeans, a loose-fitting white tee shirt, and black flip-flops. The woman looked at Danika with an ease that appeared to say, "I'm here now, you can relax," causing Danika to sigh involuntarily. Several colorful tattoos covered each forearm, but Danika couldn't quite make out what they were. The woman's dark russet hair was long, and she wore a single braid that almost reached the small of her back. Her hair framed her oval face and accentuated her high cheekbones. As she walked into the kitchen, Danika felt herself blush a more profound and deeper crimson. The woman's gaze remained on Danika, causing Danika to fidget in her seat. If the woman noticed her blushing, she only acknowledged it with a slight tilt of the head, making Danika feel as though for all her steadiness, the woman held a great many secrets locked inside and counted this moment as perhaps one more in a long line.

"Hi everyone," the woman said, her voice steady and low, vibrating enough to cause Danika to shift in her seat like a fault-line had opened up beneath them.

Chef Servante piped up. "Hi there. No worries. We were just getting started." He looked down at a sheet of paper in front of him on the worktable. "You must be Finn?"

"Yes," she nodded. "That's right. Finn Gerard."

"Welcome, Finn. Why don't you take a seat over there?" Chef Servante pointed to an open seat at the end of a large work-table in front of Danika's. Finn moved by her with ease. As Finn passed, Danika involuntarily closed her eyes and inhaled deeply. She smelled lilac, sunshine, and the faintly salty smell of ocean spray on a windy day. When Danika opened her eyes, she saw that Finn had taken her place, but had turned her head as if to continue eye contact for as long as possible.

If the atmosphere of a room changed merely by a person's presence, it did when Finn Gerard walked into that brightly lit restaurant kitchen. Danika sensed a definitive shift in the air pressure, in the temperature, in the quality of air she breathed. Her palms were suddenly sweaty, leaving hand-printed steam marks on the stainless-steel table. Danika guessed Finn to be in her early forties. She didn't look like everyone else. Actually, she didn't look like anyone else. Danika silently wondered of Finn was Native American. Simply put, she was unlike anyone Danika had ever come in contact with in her entire life. There was a part of Danika, an aspect to herself that she had never really known or had even come into contact with, that wanted to pull Finn by the hand to a quiet corner of the restaurant and say, "Did you feel what I did then? Can we spend more time together? You made me feel alive for an instant." But Danika said none of those things. Instead, she felt mildly embarrassed imagining what she must look like to Finn: an older, chubby woman, blushing at a pretty woman in a cooking class.

Chef Servante cleared his throat, forcing Danika to grudgingly shift her attention to him. He began again, "This is our first-ever Italian culinary series here at the Riverside Café. I wanted to do something like this for ages, and I'm happy to have you all in our kitchen for the next five Mondays. As you know, our restaurant is closed Monday nights. This gives us all the time in the world to prepare and enjoy a delicious meal together. I intentionally wanted this to be a small group of ten people to make the most of our time. Let's begin by going around the room and introducing ourselves. Tell me your name, where you're from and a little about why you're taking this class." He pointed to a woman at the opposite end of Danika's table to begin.

"Hello. My name is Georgette. I live in Nyack and love Italian food. I also love your restaurant, Chef Servante." The portly woman in her sixties, with short gray hair, blushed, then continued. "Anyway, I cook a lot at home for my husband, but at my age, I've found that I'm in a rut of cooking the same things over and over again."

A short, wiry woman also in her sixties spoke next. "Hi, everyone. I'm Riley. Georgette is my good friend, and we decided to take the class together. I confess, I don't cook much and doubt

I'll be much help in this class, but I love to eat!" She patted her thin belly. Everyone chuckled.

Suddenly, Danika realized she was next to introduce herself. She wasn't sure how much time had even elapsed. It was almost as if time stopped the moment Finn opened the kitchen doors.

Danika began to speak, but her voice wavered slightly when Finn turned once again to look at her. Danika felt a blush surge up from the base of her neck to the top of her hairline. The hair stood up on her forearms and along the back of her neck as if some magnetic force was drawing her very being in a different direction. Danika felt as though she was standing naked in front of these people doing the chicken dance.

"Um, hi. My name is Danika Russo. I've never taken a cooking class before, but I love to cook, and apparently love to eat a little more than Riley over here." Danika said, patting her significantly larger and rounder belly. Everyone laughed. Danika briefly looked up at Finn, whose eyes were shining on her. Danika felt her breath catch in her throat. "Okay, thanks."

Danika felt lightheaded and completely missed the introductions of the next five people. She heard talking, then some laughter, and she attempted to smile in all the right places, but she wasn't paying attention to anything except the eye-catching woman with the long braid in front of her, off to the right. Everyone's voices seemed muffled like Danika was under water holding her breath, hearing conversations on the surface in that indecipherable Peanuts-teacher-talking kind of way. Once or twice, she caught herself staring down at Finn's round and ample behind before cursing herself and returning her gaze to something less, well, less appealing.

She jolted into crystal-clear consciousness when Finn began to speak. "Hi again. I'm Finn Gerard. I recently moved to Piermont from Malibu, California. I don't know much about Italian cooking, but I'm excited to learn. Well, honestly, I'm just excited to eat." Everyone laughed.

Danika caught herself thinking about all the things she wanted to learn about Finn, mainly how she tasted. The mere thought of tasting Finn, in any number of ways, caused a surge of energy to bloom in Danika's belly and rise up to her temples. She gulped in the air like a fish out of water and tried to keep her focus on the chef, which was becoming more difficult by the minute.

CHAPTER NINE

After the introductions, Chef Servante outlined the menu. "Tonight," he said, "we're going to take it easy and get to know one another. I promise I won't make you do anything too tricky. If you'd rather watch and not participate, that's fine also. We want you to enjoy the experience and not pray for it to end!

"True Italian food begins with a simple question: what is in season? And right now, particularly with some of the wonderful local farms in our area, we are blessed with a variety of incredible, fresh ingredients. So, I've chosen three relatively simple dishes. We will begin with beet Carpaccio accompanied by arugula, radishes, and grapefruit. For our main course, we'll make squash blossom pizza." At the word pizza, virtually everyone in the room oohed and ahhed. "Finally, we'll end with a cardamom Panna Cotta with honeyed figs."

"As with most dinners, we will begin by preparing dessert since the Panna Cotta takes about sixty minutes to set with our blast chillers. Most residential refrigerators will take around two hours, so plan accordingly if you decide to make this at your next dinner party." Chef Servante handed out recipe cards that everyone passed down the line. Next, the chef strode over to the walk-in refrigerator and pulled out a large hotel pan full of ingredients. Danika noticed immediately how efficient the chef was. Movement in the kitchen wasn't wasted.

"Rather than having you all make this, I'll demonstrate the Panna Cotta. Once we're done with it, we can begin with appetizer and main course, which you'll help with."

The chef organized the ingredients whipping cream, sugar, vanilla, cardamom, figs, and honey in front of him. He opened a bottle of Riesling. "Would you mind pouring some for everyone?" he said to Georgette who promptly rose to oblige. He quickly quartered five figs and tossed them onto a platter. He drizzled honey over the top and passed the platter down the line. "No reason why you can't taste some of these incredible ingredients while we work! For me, that's always the best part." The chef laughed, and the class did too. "You know, Rieslings sometimes get a bad rap for being too sweet, but you can choose one of the more complex vintages such as from the Alsace region or even the Columbia Valley in Washington. You can choose a semisweet or dry wine that's still floral, but will feature citrus and mineral aromas and flavors which won't overpower the delicate sweetness of the fig."

One of the man-bun men chimed up, "But isn't this an Italian cooking class? Why are we tasting a German wine?" As if the man-bun wasn't enough, the comment made Danika cringe and dislike the guy even more.

"You're right, we can drink Prosecco with figs, but the figs are simply a quick taste. I was saving the Prosecco for the beet Carpaccio, and honestly, I love this wine with figs. Let's not get too caught up in rules. Please. What do you taste?" he asked one of the women.

"Very sweet," she said. "Like candy."

Chef Servante smiled politely. "And you?" he asked one of the men.

"Fruity, I guess. I don't like the seeds or whatever. They get stuck in my teeth."

The platter of figs arrived in front of Danika. She took one piece of the tender, ripe fruit, laden with honey and popped it into her mouth. She closed her eyes in delight to savor it, partially because it was the first morsel of food to cross her lips since the cranberry oat cereal at breakfast. The taste exploded in her mouth, all honey-like sweetness with a subtle hint of berry and fresher shades of the fruit. She took a sip of the Riesling, able to notice the sharper citrus tang of the wine immediately.

When she opened her eyes, Chef Servante was standing in front of her, his face so close to hers their noses almost touched. Everyone in class stared at her. "Tell me," he said quietly. "Tell me what you tasted."

Danika blushed again. "Sorry." She apologized almost out of reflex, her hand immediately rising up to cover her mouth.

"Don't be sorry. I want you to think about the food you taste. Let it sink in. Experience it. Most people throw food into their mouths, inhaling it without a second thought. But you, I could tell right away, you were experiencing it. I've got to tell you—we chefs think that's as sexy as it gets."

Danika glanced over at Finn, who smiled at her with a curious expression on her face. "Well, let me start by saying I'm really, really hungry. Um, the sweetness of the honey brought out the sweetness of the fig, but I also tasted fresh light berry."

"And when you took a sip of the wine?" Chef Servante prompted her for more.

"You're right. The wine has a sharper citrus flavor that compliments the sweetness of the honey and the fig without over-powering it. All of it together tasted like a summer morning before sunrise."

"Bingo! Grazie mille. You're blessed with a palate, my dear. Some people spend years studying food to taste it the way you did. What do you do for a living, if you don't mind my asking?"

Danika fidgeted in her seat. The last thing she wanted to do was tell this room full of strangers that she delivered mail as if that would immediately prove her to be a fraud. "I'm, well, I'm recently retired."

"Good for you. That means you can focus on developing that exceptional palate. Let's get back to work!"

As Chef Servante re-focused his attention on the Panna Cotta, Danika smiled inside. It was one of the first times she had been called out in any class at any point in her life and actually had the right answer—an answer that not everyone got. Fifty-five years old, and here she was feeling like a proud first-grader who correctly answered two times five equals ten while the rest of the class struggled to count using their stubby fingers.

Suddenly, the bright kitchen lights overwhelmed Danika, their miserable fluorescent glow casting a hideous yellow ruddiness on the strangers whose faces Danika would forget the instant they were out of sight. She felt like herself pretending to be someone more intriguing, more interesting than the woman she really was, and the awareness made her a little queasy. She turned towards Finn, who looked at her and not Chef Servante's demonstration. Danika looked directly into those large bronze eyes. Time stopped again, all the noise in the room silenced. Finn tilted her head, her lips turned up ever-so-slightly, her eyebrows tilted in an expression of curiosity, of open interest, or something else Danika couldn't quite place but now desperately wanted to know for sure.

CHAPTER TEN

The rest of the class passed by in a blur of chopping, cutting, tasting, seasoning, eating and drinking, and most of all, trying to concentrate despite the constant pull to look at Finn. Danika drank more wine in three hours of this class than she had in the three months prior. Of all three dishes, the golden beet Carpaccio was her favorite. The combination of the peppery arugula and crisp, zesty radish with the sweeter, mellow flavor of the fresh beets, and the earthy snap peas, was incredible. If the figs and honey tasted like a summer morning, the beet Carpaccio tasted like a breezy, almost hot and sunny, mid-summer day, with the punch of a grapefruit kicker.

Chef Servante explained the concept of culinary dissonance, which mesmerized Danika. He said, "Bitterness can be a turn-off on the palate. Bitterness is dissonance. The key is finding balance. The bitterness makes the good flavors taste better. It elevates flavor if done right." He had her at dissonance.

The squash blossom pizza was her least favorite. Like everyone else, she loved a good pizza, but it didn't work for her. The Chianti had worked fine for her, though. The Panna Cotta melted in her mouth and immediately became one of those bucket-list desserts she'd order if she ever found herself on death row ready to receive her final meal. It was that good.

After class as everyone filed out, Chef Servante placed his hand gently on Danika's shoulder, stopping her. "What did you think of the pizza?" he asked, his eyes bright.

"Well, I liked it. But it wasn't my favorite."

"Why not?" he asked, staring at her intently.

"I love squash blossoms. We go way back. My grandmother used to make these fritters that you'd kill someone for. But I thought the red sauce and the onion overpowered the delicate flavor of the squash blossom. I only tasted onions on the pizza when I really wanted to taste my grandmother's squash blossoms," she admitted honestly.

"Danika, I hope you don't mind me asking this, but would you be interested in coming to the restaurant more often? We're always testing new recipes before we change our menus and I need a palate like yours to run things by. I mean it when I tell you it's a gift that few people possess."

Danika's eyes widened in shock. "You know, I've been coming to your restaurant for years. I watched you on *Iron Chef Gauntlet* and everything. I can't see how you'd need someone like me around." The moment it came out of her mouth, Danika was frustrated with herself and her constant ability to minimize her strengths, as if showcasing them was somehow a liability.

Chef Servante wouldn't take no for an answer. He shook his head vehemently. "People like you are few and far between. Look at it this way: writers need good readers and editors to review their books before printing them. It's the same way for chefs. Sometimes we get too close to a recipe, and we don't taste what's right in front of us. I'd pay you, of course."

"You're feeding me. Why would you need to pay me on top of that?" Danika asked, incredulous.

"Because your skill has value. How about you come by next Monday around noon? We usually spend Mondays testing recipes since we're closed for the day. You'll get a chance to meet everyone, too."

"I don't know what to say," Danika replied.

"*Bene*. It's settled then. Hold on *un minuto*." Chef Servante ran to the walk-in. He continued talking to her, but Danika didn't understand a thing he said inside the large refrigerator. He returned with a small parcel wrapped in paper. "Vino!" He bolted off in a different direction. *This is ridiculous*, thought Danika, but she secretly enjoyed every minute of it.

He returned a moment later with a bottle of wine. He handed Danika the parcel and the wine.

"What's this?" Danika asked.

"Summer truffle from Umbria called *scorzone*. And, in my opinion, the perfect wine for truffles. It's a 2001 Ceretto Bricco Roche Barolo." He kissed his fingers and raised his hand in the air. "Perfecto, but different from the white truffles of Piedmont harvested in September."

"Chef, I can't accept this. First of all, I don't know the first thing about cooking truffles. Second, I know what you handed me is probably really expensive. And the wine is seventeen years old. It can't be cheap either."

"Bella, bella, *state zitte*. Be quiet. It's my gift. Please. It's part of your new education. You must try things, taste them, experience them. Then we talk. This is how it will be. Now, to be clear, you do not cook these truffles. Do you have a mandoline?"

Danika nodded. "A cheap one."

"Shave them over scrambled eggs, over asparagus, vegetables, risotto. The truffle has a remarkable flavor that doesn't taste like anything else, it is capable of transforming a simple recipe into something memorable. These are summer truffles. Much less intense, with a strong perfume. Now, the wine. That must be allowed to breathe for at least two hours. Decant it. And please, by all means, call me Tony." He smiled broadly.

Danika nodded. Her new culinary education was apparently underway. "Tony. Alright. I don't know what to say. This is more than I bargained for!"

"Ah, one more thing. Make sure to eat that truffle by tomorrow. You must eat it fresh."

"Tony, look at me. Do you honestly think this is going to sit around in my fridge for long?" Danika laughed as Tony hugged her.

When Danika exited the restaurant at nearly nine o'clock in the evening, she wasn't even aware of her feet hitting the ground. Earlier in the day before class, she fretted about trying something new, if she would fit in or feel comfortable. In the span of the first cooking class, she'd learned that she possessed a hidden talent and now had a job tasting food at her favorite restaurants. To top it off, she met someone new who stirred things in her nether-regions that she thought were long past stirring.

She clicked the unlock button on her pickup and heard the *"cheep, cheep"* of the alarm disarming. As she stepped up into the cab, she heard, "Hi, excuse me. You're Danika, right?"

Danika left the wine and truffle on the driver's seat and stepped back down. She turned to see Finn smiling at her and the discomfort that she'd begun to feel comfortable with rebounded.

"Hi. Yes. I'm Danika. You're Finn?"

"That's me," Finn replied, her voice low.

"Your name is unusual," commented Danika. "What's it short for?"

"Finlandia."

Danika regarded Finn with a blank expression on her face.

"You know, the vodka? My mom was an alcoholic. I'm pretty sure she got Finn from Finlandia vodka, but she didn't live long enough for me to ask her." Finn chuckled.

That wasn't the answer Danika expected. She was tongue-tied and had no idea where to go with this conversation next.

"Right, sorry. Too much information. Anyway. I guess I'll see you next week at class," stammered Finn.

Something in the air shifted between them as if they were both signing a contract without reading the fine print. Danika took a deep breath, trying to find a space inside her that wasn't off balance, that was sure-footed and true like Finn seemed to be.

Danika pulled the bottle of wine and truffle off of her seat and showed them to Finn. "So, I have these. Care to try them with me? I've never used truffles before and I'm a little intimidated." Danika wanted to say that she was intimidated by Finn. She wished to pull her close and feel some of that certainty that effortlessly flowed out from Finn. Danika wanted to ask Finn if Finn felt the pull in the air between them. But, she only held out the paper bag of truffles and wine like a peace offering at the first Thanksgiving.

Finn stepped in closer to peer at the wine label. "That's like a two-hundred-dollar bottle of wine, you know."

"It is?" Danika raised her eyebrows in surprise. She knew it was pricey, but she had no idea it was that expensive. "Wow. Well, care to drink it with me tomorrow?" *Care to lie with me under the stars and hold me to keep me from flying away?* Danika thought to herself.

Finn smiled. Danika's heart raced. Although it was after nine o'clock in the evening with the sun nearly set, the light that radiated from within Finn's eyes seemed to light up Danika's face and the entire sidewalk. "I'd like that very much," Finn said. "Where should we meet?"

"Well, you can come to my new place. I just moved in. What's your cell number? I'll text you the address and directions. It gets a little tricky because I'm off a dirt road. I doubt it will come up on your navigation system." Danika forced herself to slow down. She pulled her cell phone out of her pocket and punched in the numbers as Finn recited them. She typed a quick text to Finn with Hi. It's Danika. "There. That's me."

"Great. What time? How about six o'clock?" suggested Danika, shocked she was inviting this woman to her RV. In the moment, it seemed like the most reasonable thing in the world.

"Since I can't bring wine, what would you like me to bring?"

"Nothing but yourself," Danika replied, smiling. She didn't want to stop talking to Finn or looking at her. A car whizzed by breaking the moment and the energy that flowed between them. Finn stepped back. Danika felt the warmth of her eyes fade into the oncoming night.

"See you tomorrow," Finn said then waved again, and Danika reciprocated as she climbed into her pickup truck and closed the door. Danika took longer than necessary to start the truck and put it into gear because she became sidetracked watching Finn walk across the street to her silver Subaru Forrester. Danika's heart beat so heavy in her chest she heard it reverberate in her ears.

CHAPTER ELEVEN

"Wait. Tell me this again," Natalie said, as she leaned forward in her Adirondack chair. Danika skimmed rocks across the surface of the pond on a bright, hot, and humid Tuesday, the morning after the first cooking class, and the morning of her first date in a very long time.

"Nat, I'm not telling you the same story for the third time. I've told you every minute detail that I can remember."

"Mmm-hmm, you certainly did." Natalie leaned back in the chair, clasping her hands behind her head as she looked up at the sky. She laughed to herself, shaking her head in amazement. "Remember that day we sat in your parents' house making that list? If you had told me then that you'd sell everything, buy a kick-ass RV, land it here in this enchanted place, then go to that cooking class and have a freaking Iron Chef tell you that you have an amazing palate, *and* offer you a job tasting *his* food..." Natalie's voice trailed off. She shook her head again in wonder.

"Don't forget the best part," Danika quipped as she plopped down in the seat next to Natalie.

"And what might that be? The two-hundred-dollar bottle of

wine, the fresh truffles from Italy, or the date the next night with the hot chick with the cool name who makes your heart go all pitter-patter?" Natalie smiled. Danika smiled back. It all sounded surreal.

"I know. It's hard to say which is the coolest, but I might have to go with the pitter-patter part."

"Mmm-hmm, yeah you do!"

"In all seriousness, help. I haven't had an actual date in a long time. I don't know what to do. I shouldn't have asked her over so quickly. I should've given myself more time."

"Time? You don't need more time. Woman, the last time you had a date, George H.W.Bush was still president." Natalie snickered at her own joke.

"Um, not helpful. Not helpful at all. What do I do?"

"What do you mean what do you do? You savor every drop of the wine, shave fresh truffle all over her naked body, and slowly eat those decadent little pieces off her."

Danika had to admit that idea was more than a little appealing. "You know what I mean."

"No, actually, I don't. Be yourself. You are a smart, funny, wonderful woman. If she has half a brain, she will see that. You got the vibe from her, right?"

"What? You mean gay-dar? Jesus, Natalie, I don't even know if I have gay-dar installed on this old operating system. I mean, I guess yes, but I'm not going into this with any assumptions. Maybe she'll be a new friend," Danika mused.

"You're overdue for an upgrade to your operating system. And yeah, a friend you want to lick summer truffles off of. Don't try too hard. This place is magnificent. You have plenty to talk about there. Keep it light, and for God's sake, don't get into the sad sack details of Angela or your dad. Nothing too heavy. Play some music, let her talk, go skinny dipping. Enjoy the time with an attractive woman," Natalie concluded in her bossy tone.

Danika glanced at her watch. "I don't mean to throw you out, but I'm throwing you out. I've got a shower to take, wine to figure out how to decant in something more suitable than a plastic pitcher, and an outfit to select."

"Don't forget to trim your fingernails. He-he."

"Oh, shut up. Get out of here." Danika slapped Natalie on her behind as she headed for the Prius.

"Have fun! Call me tomorrow!" Natalie waved and drove off.

Danika sat by the pond for a few minutes in a feeble attempt to settle her nerves. She saw a red-tailed hawk fly overhead and land on a massive oak tree off to the south. All of the other birds suddenly became scarce as they hid out from the hawk's shadow. She wondered how long she'd been hiding out under the shadow of one thing, or person, or another. She spent the better part of her life hiding out from her true self. First, she hid from her parents; then she morphed into other people for the few other lovers she had before Angela. At the beginning of her relationship with Angela, it felt authentic; she felt present. But it wasn't long before Angela's energy sucked all of Danika's identity down some insatiable black hole. Angela's illness and her father's illness were the last two stops on the train of her life that never really stopped anywhere she wanted to go.

This was different. Maybe it was this place, and how she found it. Or, perhaps it was the freedom that her parents' death, and Angela's death, finally provided. She was a smart enough woman to realize all of those things had an impact on where she was right in this very instant. For the first time in years, she sat back and centered her mind on one thought: Focus on what you feel.

She felt good. She felt alive. She felt excited about the possibility of something with Finn that she wasn't able to place or didn't entirely understand. She felt nervous, the kind of apprehension that comes from stepping in the right direction, not down the wrong path. She had a hunch this was going to be an enjoyable evening. After a quick check of her watch, she jumped into action.

She set up a fire in the fire pit thanks to all the wood and kindling already stacked by the shed. If the rain held off and the breeze stuck around, they might be able to sit outside by a fire. Danika was also happy the solar lights arrived from Amazon yesterday. Now she had low lights around the fire pit and from the parking area to the door of the trailer, which really helped considering there were no street lights or area lights except the RV's LED-lit awning. The solar lights automatically kicked on and off at dawn and dusk.

Danika walked into the RV and did a quick look-around. Satisfied it appeared clean and neat, she set out dishes and napkins, and wine glasses. Flipping open the laptop, she settled on Michelle Malone's new album, *Sling and Arrows*, wanting to listen to something a little sexy with a rock vibe. Once Michelle's soulful voice filled the space with "Sugar on My Tongue," she conducted a quick Google search for "how to decant wine." At least she did the first part right without even knowing it. She'd kept the bottle upright on the counter since last night, allowing the sediment to settle to the bottom. Next, she looked around her kitchen and found a narrow glass pitcher. This would have to do. She carefully uncorked the bottle and slowly began pouring the wine into the pitcher, cautious not to disturb the sediment or pour it into the pitcher.

With that part complete, she washed asparagus and removed the burrata cheese from the refrigerator, along with a half-dozen farm-fresh eggs, allowing them to come to room temperature. Next, she settled on making a fragrant, light pesto to serve with the burrata and fresh baguette. Before rinsing a bunch of fresh basil, she held it to her nose, inhaling the aromatic pepper mixed with a mint scent. The smell of basil always reminded Danika of her grandfather who used to keep a sprig tucked behind an ear in the summer.

She tore the bunch in half and threw it in the food processor. Next, she took two cloves of garlic into her hands. She tossed one back into the clay garlic pot, opting to go a little lighter on the garlic in case a kiss was in her future. The mere thought of kissing Finn made Danika a little dizzy, causing her to chuckle at herself. Having a crush was a new sensation. Re-focusing her thoughts to the task at hand, she smashed the side of her chef's knife over the garlic, allowing her to quickly pull the papery covering away from the clove. Into the food processor went the garlic clove. She threw a large handful of pine nuts in a small sauté pan on the stove. Once they were golden and toasted, she dropped them into the food processor. Finally, she grated about a half-cup of Parmigiano Reggiano cheese, and threw it into the processor as well. As the processor whirled, she drizzled a half cup of olive oil until the mixture emulsified. Once or twice she scraped down the sides of the food processor to make sure she got all of it mixed. After transferring the pesto to a small bowl, Danika tasted the pesto. She added kosher salt and fresh ground pepper and tasted again. One more pinch of salt and it was perfect.

Satisfied, she cleaned all her utensils, and the food processor, and made her way into the bedroom. Her closet was small, so the options were limited. She didn't feel like wearing shorts. Instead, she chose a comfortable pair of white jeans with a hole in one knee. She tried them on. They were a little snug across her midsection, but what else was new. She found a tab collar black button-down shirt that she was always fond of.

Finally, Danika got down to the business of taking an incredibly long and arduous shower where she scrubbed and shaved, loofahed, and sanded about every inch of her body until she was all pink and soft and sparkling clean. As she dressed, she began to imagine Finn unbuttoning the same buttons she was fastening.

The same queasy feeling rose in her belly. She looked at her reflection in the mirror and wasn't entirely satisfied. She turned sideways and tried to square her shoulders and suck her stomach in. After a few seconds, she blew out her breath. Her belly fell back into place. She sighed. Finn would arrive any minute, making it too late for any miraculous weight loss formula.

Moments after Danika stepped down the two stairs from her bedroom, she saw Finn exit the car. She froze mid-step to watch Finn straighten her long braid. She wondered what it would be like to be naked underneath Finn, with her long hair spread out like a blanket over them both. Danika swallowed hard. A few moments later, there was a light *knock-knock* on the door.

CHAPTER TWELVE

"Hey there. You found me okay?" Danika asked, her voice wavering more than she expected. She welcomed Finn up the steps of the trailer that suddenly felt too small to hold them both. Finn carried a small platter covered in aluminum foil and a large bunch of fresh flowers. Danika took the flowers out of her hand because the flowers blocked Finn's face. An awkward moment passed where they might've hugged hello if not for the flowers and platter in between them. Danika inhaled and smelled lilacs and beach. Her stomach flipped.

"Hi. These are for you. I know you told me not to bring anything, but I can't come empty-handed, so I baked brownies." Finn said, her voice low and steady.

Danika tried to peek underneath the foil, but Finn lightly smacked Danika's hand away, to Danika's surprise. "No peeking!" Finn commanded.

"Please come in. I'm sure this isn't exactly what you expected," Danika said, motioning with her hand in the air. Yesterday she was proud of her RV and the home she created. Here with

Finn, Danika felt like some ratty trailer-park trash. She resisted the urge to run away and hide in the bushes.

Finn looked around. If she thought less of Danika for owning a trailer, she did not show it. "No, but it's amazing. The property is spectacular. I've never been in a trailer this nice before."

Danika hunted for a vase. She knew she had one somewhere. "Take a look around while I get these beautiful flowers in some water."

Finn slowly walked around the living space of the trailer. She stopped to look out Danika's favorite picture window, which had a perfect view of the fire pit and pond. Danika wondered if Finn stood long enough, would she sprout roots out her feet and remain there forever?

After a few moments, Finn slowly walked up the two stairs to the bathroom and into the bedroom. Every movement Finn made was deliberate as if she always knew where her feet would land without even looking. At the sight of Finn walking into her bedroom, Danika's breath caught in her throat.

"Wow. It's bigger than it looks from the outside. The bathroom is huge. So is the bedroom. I can see why this is appealing. It's a perfect amount of space, and you can move it wherever you want," mused Finn as she returned to the kitchen area.

"Well, that was the plan, but this is the first and only place it's ever been parked. I bought it a month ago and moved out here like a week ago It's all still pretty new."

"What do you do for laundry? Do you have to take it into town?"

"No, I have a stackable washer dryer in the bedroom wardrobe a bit smaller than residential units, but they work great."

Finn paused for a moment, openly staring at Danika with those ever-luminescent eyes. Danika tried to keep herself engaged with the flowers. Otherwise, she was going to plant one on Finn so fast Finn wouldn't know what hit her.

"So, would you like some of this expensive wine that I decanted?" Danika motioned to the pitcher of wine, smiling.

Finn hesitated. "A glass of ice water would be great," she said, making Danika wonder if Finn was as nervous as she was.

"Water coming right up," Danika said lightly.

"Can you show me around the property?" Finn asked as she returned to the kitchen area, her eyes suddenly clouded over as if hiding something she was not prepared for Danika to see.

"Sure." Danika poured and handed Finn a large tumbler of ice water and prepared one for herself. "I'll show you around the pond. It's my favorite time of day out here."

They exited the trailer and walked around by the fire pit. Danika forced herself to slow down to Finn's steady pace, and the result instantly relaxed her. Finn commented, "The view is incredible. You don't have any neighbors. I bet the stars are bright here at night."

"They are! Although it has been pretty buggy at night so I don't usually survive for long."

"When the weather changes, the bugs will vanish, and you'll have this fire pit. I bet you'll use it all winter."

"I hope so." *I hope to be sitting by a fire with you as the snow falls around us*, Danika thought.

"What kind of wildlife have you seen? I'm sure you'll have plenty of deer and fox, probably coyote too," mused Finn aloud. They sat down on the Adirondack chairs overlooking the pond. Finn rubbed her right thigh in a circular pattern that made Danika's mouth go dry.

"Let's see, so far, I've only seen deer, birds, opossum, skunk, and a huge hawk. No coyote yet." Danika took a long sip of water.

"How did you find this place?" Finn asked.

"It's a long story. I recently sold my parents' old house in

Nyack and always wanted an RV, so much so that I decided to pull the trigger before I thought through where I'd put it. Luckily, one of my former co-workers, also a dear friend, knew the guy who owned this property. The owner had it all set up for a trailer, but he got a divorce and found a new job in Colorado, so I got lucky. I can stay here virtually rent-free for as long as I want. My friend, Pete, thinks the guy will end up selling me the property after a year or two of being out in Colorado." While Danika spoke, she noticed how intently Finn gazed at her, as if every word she said was notable. It was simultaneously unsettling and reassuring. It made Danika feel like she was going too fast, skimming over too much of what she really wanted to share.

"It's incredible. Especially around here where everyone is on top of one another in one subdivision after another," Finn said, in a tone that Danika thought contained a dose of repugnance.

"You're not from around here, are you?" Danika asked lightly, recalling Finn telling the cooking group she grew up in Malibu, California. The light blue, late day sky was swirled with high clouds like cotton balls that had been pulled taut. Her grandfather taught her that those clouds were called "mare's tails" and they usually meant rain was near. The cicadas were in full force, providing a humming backdrop to their conversation. A light breeze turned the leaves on the trees upside down, another sign that rain or a storm was on its way.

"No. Can you tell? I don't exactly fit in the whole New York suburban scene. I grew up at the beach in Malibu, California."

"Malibu, wow. Isn't that where all those rich Hollywood people live?" Danika asked.

"Pretty much. My dad was a film editor, so we fit the bill, I guess. Growing up on the beach is a different way of life. Here, you have this big old river, but no one can swim in it because it's filled with too many pollutants, so that you can look but you but you can't touch it. I'm not a big fan." Finn's disdain was evident.

"What brought you to New York if you love Malibu so much?"

Finn hesitated. "That's a long story," she said.

"Well, the beach isn't too far away," Danika said, trying to lighten up Finn's waning mood.

Finn scoffed. "Are you kidding me? I tried it once. I took a ride to Fire Island. What a nightmare. Hours in traffic to find a beach so jammed with people that they blocked the view of the water. No. That's not the kind of beach where I grew up. I'd literally hop on my bike and be on this spectacular beach with hardly any people on it in like five minutes."

"That sounds amazing, and a lot like Provincetown, where I've spent a lot of time over the years."

"I've never been to Provincetown, but I heard it's great. It's definitely on my list to visit," Finn replied.

"If you like deserted beaches, you'll love Provincetown," Danika said as she tried to imagine Finn lying naked in the sand, but she was unable to conjure up a clear picture of the landscape. Imagining Finn naked was much less challenging.

"You looked pretty then. What were you thinking about?" Finn said quickly, jolting Danika back to the present. Their eyes locked for a fleeting moment, and Danika thought she caught Finn mid-blush. Danika broke their eye contact first. It was too intense, too powerful, and it scared Danika nearly out of her own skin.

Danika was mortified. "Um, well I was trying to imagine you on the beach in Malibu, but I've never been there, and don't know what it looks like." Danika decided to keep the *Finn lying naked on the beach* part to herself.

"Whatever you were imagining made your whole face light up," Finn pressed, smiling. "You're beautiful when you smile." Finn's voice vibrated low; the timbre rumbled in Danika's belly.

Danika felt the blush rise from her neck to her ears. She had it on the tip of her tongue to ask Finn if she was a lesbian. She was definitely getting that vibe from Finn. Her game was more than a little rusty, but to Danika, it felt a lot like Finn was flirting with her. She opted to leave the question be for a while and see if Finn might talk more about her background. "Let's go back inside. It's getting a little buggy," Danika suggested as she swatted a mosquito on her neck. "I'm getting hungry too. Are you ready for some wine now?" Danika stood. Finn nodded and did the same.

Finn stepped forward, and for a split second, Danika thought Finn would kiss her. Their eyes locked again. The butterflies in Danika's stomach flapped around something fierce, and she had no idea how to stop it. In her whole life, she'd never felt anything like this. She was completely unprepared. She inhaled and held her breath, sure Finn saw her heart bouncing out of her chest. Very gently, Finn stretched her right arm out and pulled something out of Danika's hair. Her touch was light and quick, but their eyes remained locked until Finn pulled away. The breeze blew around them more insistent, and the sky had begun to turn from light blue to a light yellowish green.

"Uh, you had something in your hair," Finn nearly whispered.

Danika looked down briefly at Finn's fingers. She didn't see anything, unsure if Finn made up a reason to get close. Danika cleared her throat. "Um, shall we?" She began walking back to the RV, knowing Finn was flirting with her. Now if she could only remember how to flirt back!

CHAPTER THIRTEEN

Once inside, Danika busied herself with appetizer preparation, trying not to openly stare at Finn, who was still mysterious to Danika and difficult to figure out. Normally, Danika possessed the ability to size-up someone new quickly, but with Finn, she found herself feeling as though she was trying to see Finn through a mysterious haze. "What can I do?" Finn asked, leaning over the other side of the narrow center island, fracturing Danika's tenuous concentration.

Danika pointed to her laptop on the table. "Well, first you can pick us some music. My iTunes is open. After that, why don't you pour us some wine while I make the appetizer?" When Finn turned her back on Danika to flip open the laptop on the small dining table, Danika stopped for a moment to admire the woman standing across from her whom she barely knew. Finn wasn't traditionally beautiful. The word was on the tip of Danika's tongue. As she sliced the fresh baguette on a bias, the word came to her. *Alluring.* Finn was alluring. Her presence, her energy, her husky voice, strong jawline, full lips, that braid, her tattoos, those eyes—all of it formed a captivating package.

Danika flipped on a couple of lights. The sky outside had begun to darken much earlier than normal.

"Wow. You have a ton of music," Finn commented, turning her head to look at Danika. "Like a lot. Your library is really varied. You go from Duncan Sheik to Eminem and the Cranberries. Very cool."

"I listened to a lot of music for my job," Danika responded.

"Oh? The job you retired from?"

"Yep. Thirty years of doing the same thing day in and day out," declared Danika.

"Which was?" Finn asked.

"I delivered mail," stated Danika matter-of-factly, hoping to get it out and over with quickly to minimize her embarrassment. She wanted to be able to say she was a doctor or a lawyer, something compelling to elicit an impressed response. Instead, Danika told Finn that she'd been a mail carrier. She half expected Finn to run out of the RV laughing at her and the utter failure of her very life.

Finn stopped looking at the laptop and stared at Danika. "You did that for thirty years?? Holy crap. Wait. How old are you? Sorry, that was abrupt. You don't have to answer that," Finn said quickly.

Danika laughed. "That's okay. I'm fifty-five. My birthday is coming up next week, actually." *Great. Let's get it all out on the table,* Danika thought wryly.

"A Cancer?"

Danika nodded.

"No way you are fifty-five. You look much younger," Finn exclaimed. "I mean, I assumed we were the same age."

"How old are you?" Danika asked carefully.

"I turned forty in May. I'm a Taurus. I was ten years old when you started your job. How weird is that?" Finn asked, her eyes wide.

"Weird," Danika stated flatly. Being reminded of her A.A.R.P. status wasn't exactly a turn-on.

Finn stared again at Danika. "I mean it; you look much younger."

Danika chuckled. She thought back to that night in her parents' bathroom when she gave herself a full-body once-over and shivered slightly at the thought. "Well, if you'd met me two months ago, I doubt you'd say the same thing."

Finn didn't pursue the topic. She shifted gears. "Who is Brandi Carlile? You have a ton of her music."

"Play her. You'll see why she's one of my favorites, Danika answered as she sliced the fresh baguette in half-inch sections on a bias. In a moment, Brandi Carlile's sultry voice filled the space. Finn tipped her head back to listen. The two were silent for a few moments as they took in the music.

"Her voice is soulful, raw, and tender, all at once," Finn remarked.

That impressed Danika. "Exactly why I love her. One second she's a female Johnny Cash rocking it out, the next, it's a quiet, tender moment of pure authenticity."

Finn sat down at a barstool across from her. "What are you making over here? You've been very busy."

"This isn't any big complicated menu. I stopped at this wonderful dairy farm this morning and saw they made a fresh batch of burrata cheese, which is ridiculously creamy. So, I decided on burrata with fresh pesto on a baguette. I'm hoping it holds up to the wine and will be a good start before our truffle extravaganza."

Finn jumped up. "Right! The wine!"

Danika laughed. Finn poured a half glass for both of them as Danika placed the bread, bright green pesto, and the burrata in front of them.

"How do we eat this? I don't think I've ever had burrata

cheese. What's it like? It looks like mozzarella to me." Finn peered down at the cheese.

Danika explained, "It is similar. It's a lot creamier. It's like a package with a present inside. You'll see." Danika took her knife and cut the room-temperature burrata in two. A gooey, white, creamy mess oozed out from within. "Burrata is filled with thick, fresh cream, and tiny shreds of stretched mozzarella curd that spill out when the magic ball is broken."

Finn smiled, looking intently at the cheese, then at Danika. "How do we eat it?" She asked, her eyes blazing on Danika in a way that made Danika feel she wasn't exactly talking about the food.

"I'll show you." Danika took the pesto and poured it over the cut open burrata. She took a piece of baguette and scooped up a spoonful of cheese and pesto, placing it on the slice of baguette. The effect was a beautiful package of the crusty baguette and white cheese, topped by the bright pesto.

"It looks too pretty to eat," Finn remarked as Danika placed it on a small plate and slid it over to her along with a napkin. She then made one for herself.

Danika raised her glass in a toast and Finn did the same. "What are we toasting?" Finn asked. Danika felt the smooth surface of the center island counter with the palm of her hand. The island separated her body from Finn's, and it was too much. Danika walked around the island, moving closer to be face-to-face with Finn, less than a foot apart. Danika sighed.

"Here's to possibilities," stated Danika, her eyes locked on Finn's.

"To possibilities," Finn responded, holding Danika's gaze. They both sniffed the Barolo, then took a sip. Finn closed her eyes for a moment while Danika swallowed the wine. "It's delicious," Finn declared.

"It really is. "I can smell anise and spice, and the taste is really fresh and vibrant, but then again I wouldn't know how it really compares to a ten-dollar bottle."

Next, Finn took a bite of the baguette. "This is ridiculous. Now I know why you like that cheese. What else can you do with it?"

"Burrata? Well, you can eat it with fresh heirloom tomatoes, drizzle it with olive oil and coarse sea salt. It even goes well on pizza, but you have to put the cheese on after you take the pizza out of the oven. You don't cook it. Honestly, I think this is the best way to eat it." *I can spread it on my body, and you can get creative,* Danika thought. Danika took a bite and closed her eyes. She loved the nutty, grassy pesto that ended with a zing of garlic. She adored the creamy burrata and the crunch from the baguette. This was of her favorite summertime meals.

Danika opened her eyes to Finn staring at her. "There is nothing sexier than watching a beautiful woman enjoy great food," said Finn quietly, her lips turned up, her high cheekbones flushed pink. If Danika wondered about Finn's sexuality before, she no longer questioned it. That line was a flashing neon sign reading *Lesbian. Lesbian. Lesbian.*

Danika leaned forward. Finn leaned forward. Their lips were inches apart. Danika smelled that same lilac and salt-spray ocean combination on Finn as she had the first night of cooking class. It was more intoxicating than the wine. She tilted her head. Finn came close. Observing Finn's lowered lids and long lashes while Finn studied her mouth sent a wave of something entirely new through Danika's body. She felt Finn's breath and heard her own heart beating in her temples. They were as close as two people could be without touching. Millimeters apart, but both held back; Danika savored the moment until it became too unbearable not to touch Finn. It was as if the Earth tilted enough off its axis to push them together.

Their lips barely touched. Danika stopped breathing. Finn's

supple lips moved, gently taking Danika's lower lip between them. Danika's body unconsciously responded. Her fingertips flew to Finn's strong jawline, caressing it. Her hips leaned forward, connecting with Finn's. They were almost the same height and fit perfectly against each other. Danika felt the heat from Finn's body coming off her like steam off a lake on a cold morning. Their kiss intensified. Danika lost herself in the kiss, in the movement of Finn's lips, the smell of her, the feel of her.

Suddenly, a massive crack of lightning lit up the sky, and the room, for an instant, as if a giant spotlight turned on from above. The flash was followed by a loud and powerful crack of thunder, shaking the RV around them. In a matter of seconds, rain poured down from the sky in torrents, nearly drowning out the music and their heavy breathing.

The funny thing was, neither of them jumped when the thunder boomed overhead as if they somehow expected it as if the weather was merely a continuation of what was passing between them. The power clicked off. The music stopped, the hum of the air conditioner ceased. The pounding rain and Danika's hammering heart were the only discernible remaining sounds. At that moment, Danika felt her old, leaden identity disappear, and in its place, someone new and lighter came forth, delivered during the raging storm.

CHAPTER FOURTEEN

Finn broke their kiss first, stepping back. Her eyelids were heavy, looking to Danika as if it was too colossal an effort for Finn to raise her gaze from Danika's mouth. "That was unexpected," Finn declared, as she sucked in a deep breath as if pulling herself back from the brink of a jagged cliff.

While the rain splattered against the top and sides of the RV, Danika became keenly aware this moment was incredibly important, as if it would somehow dictate their future. Finn's tone belied an emotion that one wouldn't typically equate with a rocking first kiss. Danika's senses were on overdrive, the pulsing in her abdomen had yet to subside, yet something about Finn's tone and the expression on her face left Danika feeling a slight, almost intangible sadness that was entirely at odds with how Danika experienced the same moment.

Danika also realized they'd been standing in darkness for a few minutes. The next crack of lightning lit up the room for a split second, allowing Danika to see Finn wipe a tear from her cheek before everything went black again. That was enough to spur Danika to action. She quickly walked around to the center island and pulled open a drawer where she felt around for a candle lighter. She moved over to the small dining table and lit a small scented candle. The single flame was just bright enough for them to see each other and their general surroundings, giving Danika the opportunity to illuminate a few other candles near the entertainment center.

As Danika moved around the room, she tried to think of what to say, or how to respond. The energy in the room felt thick like the rain had covered them in an impenetrable blanket of uncertainty. She finally spoke, saying the safest thing possible. "Good thing we're in an RV. I can fire up the generator." Danika chuckled at her own lame joke.

"No, don't," was all Finn said. "I prefer it this way. It's quiet and peaceful, I always liked candlelight." Danika wondered if she preferred to remain in darkness to keep whatever was going on inside her hidden.

"Okay," Danika said cautiously. She took her wine and sat down on the leather couch. Finn still hadn't really moved. Danika patted the seat next to her. "I don't bite," she said lightly.

Finn's expression shifted as if the thought of Danika biting her was somehow incredibly arousing. She cleared her throat and took a big gulp of wine, finally making her way over to Danika to sit down. An awkward silence ensued as the storm raged outside.

"Do you want to talk about that kiss?" Danika asked, turning to face Finn. Finn stared down at her lap as she made circles with her fingers around the rim of the wine glass. Danika leaned back, trying to give Finn space to say or feel whatever it was she needed to, but she was more than a little confused by Finn's reaction.

"No. If that's okay. I don't. I mean the kiss was amazing, and I'm having a hard time focusing on anything else but wanting to do it again. I need to take a breather here. Can we ..." Finn's voice trailed off.

Danika took Finn's hand and held it for a moment in her lap.

Finn looked into her eyes with a blazing intensity that nearly took Danika's breath away. "Finn, whatever it is you're feeling is okay. Really. We aren't teenagers. We both have pasts. I get it. I'll do my damnedest to keep my hands off you, because I do find you incredibly attractive, but we don't have to rush to bed." Danika felt Finn tense at the mere thought them being in bed together. "Why don't we take a step back and enjoy this time together. After all, I've got scrambled eggs with truffles to cook," Danika chuckled, trying desperately to lighten the mood. Like riding on a high-speed train at night, they'd both passed a point of no return, only it was Finn who appeared uncharacteristically off balance.

Finn's eyes blazed through Danika, she raised her free hand and very gently ran her fingertips across Danika's lower lip, then down to her jawline and neck, leaving Danika with a burning sensation wherever Finn's fingers made contact with her skin. It was, perhaps, the single most erotic experience of Danika's entire life. If Finn asked her to jump off a sixty-story building in that instant, Danika would have quickly obliged. "I can't believe your idea of a gourmet dinner on a first date is scrambled eggs," whispered Finn, her voice husky and teasing.

"So, this is a date, then?" Danika asked lightly, her eyebrows raised in surprise.

Finn smiled, tipping her head coyly to one side. "This doesn't feel like a date, exactly," was all she said in response.

No, it didn't, thought Danika. It felt like a homecoming, like an oasis in the middle of a desert, like waking up from a long dream. They had somehow zoomed right past a date into an utterly unfamiliar realm to Danika that she'd never experienced in any other relationship over the course of her life.

Danika pulled away and stood up; she suddenly needed some distance to stop smelling Finn's perfume to focus on something else. It was all too much to take in. She took a candle over to the center island where she focused herself on the task of making

Finn the best damned scrambled eggs of her life on the three burner propane stove. "Truffles are said to be an ancient Roman aphrodisiac," she declared, the irony more than evident.

"Great. Just what I need, more of a turnoon." Finn said dryly as she leaned back on the sofa and crossed her legs, watching Danika with an almost predatory expression that caused Danika to actually feel her pulse in between her legs.

"While I'm here slaving in relative darkness to make you dinner, since you won't let me turn on the generator, why don't you tell me more about yourself?" Danika asked.

"Like what?"

"Anything. I noticed the tattoos on your arm. What do they stand for? What do you do for a living? Do you have siblings? Favorite color? You get the idea," Danika advised as she cracked eggs over a glass bowl, tossing the shells into the sink.

"Well, as for the tattoos, I have quite a few. She showed the tattoos on one arm. Most of them are Navajo symbols back when I was going through a rough patch after my mom died." She pointed to a curved animal above her right elbow. "That's a bear. It stands for strength." She pointed to another of a bird with its wings squared and pointing downward. "That's a thunderbird, which stands for unlimited happiness. I've got the usual water, butterflies, stars, a surfboard riding a wave. Back in my twenties I was always getting tattoos. I used to be a surfing instructor before moving to New York. What else? I'm an only child. My favorite color is purple," Finn ticked off her responses.

"Why did you leave Malibu and come here, of all places?" asked Danika as she poured a few tablespoons of heavy cream into the eggs. She tried not to think of all the other tattoos on Finn's body. "I can't imagine the need for surfing instructors on the Hudson."

"That's a long story," said Finn flatly, "and a not altogether happy one."

"Ah. Okay. I get it." Danika responded cautiously. The mystery of Finn would not be solved on this night. She seasoned the eggs with a pinch of salt and a few grinds of pepper. She bent down and pulled out a medium-sized non-stick skillet and placed it on the stove. Danika diced up the raw asparagus and tossed into the pan with some butter, and dash of salt and pepper.

"No, you don't get it, but I appreciate giving me space," Finn continued. "It's been a really rough six months."

"For me, too. Why did you sign up for the cooking class? Danika asked, careful not to push too hard. She had the distinct impression that too much probing would send Finn running out into the rain.

"I have absolutely no idea. I'm really not very interested in learning to cook. It was something different and new, and I thought I needed a little of both."

"That's funny, I felt the same way," Danika mused. "I've been so stuck in a rut that I kind of forgot who I was. The cooking class seemed like a good way to make an attempt at reconnecting with myself and getting out of my comfort zone a little bit."

Danika tossed the asparagus by using a quick wrist motion to move the pan away from her. The instant the asparagus hit the edge, she did a small backward jerk, and then move the skillet forward again to catch the asparagus that had been sent upward. It was a total chef move she'd perfected over the years. Danika adjusted the flame to low. Then, she removed the truffle from the paper and smelled it, inhaling the pungent, earthy fragrance. She carefully cut a few wafer-thin truffle slices with her plastic mandoline and tossed them into the melting butter, again lowering the flame. She did not want to cook the truffle, only infuse the butter with its flavor. The room immediately smelled earthy and pungent. Heavenly.

"Wow. That smells great," Finn proclaimed. She rose and walked over to the center island, sitting down on the barstool. She made herself another burrata, baguette, and pesto bite, chewing slowly, observing as Danika cooked. "What about you? What's your story?" Finn asked, apparently attempting to steer the conversation away from herself.

"My story?" Danika hesitated. Natalie's voice popped into her head from their earlier conversation where Natalie warned Danika not to get into too many details about Angela or her dad. She poured the eggs into the skillet and gave them a light swirl with a non-stick spatula, resisting the urge to over-stir the eggs. "Let's see. I'm an only child, like you. You already know I delivered mail for thirty years before recently retiring. I told you that I grew up here. Both my parents died; my dad passed about a year ago of cancer. I sold their house and ended up here."

"I'm sorry," Finn responded.

"Don't be. We weren't close since he caught me kissing my best friend when we were teenagers. I didn't really have a loving relationship with either of them over the years."

"What about relationships?" Finn queried. Danika found it interesting that Finn wanted to talk about Danika's past, but not her own. She thought for a moment about being equally cryptic with her responses but decided that wouldn't serve much of a purpose.

"I was never a big player if that's what you're asking. I'm more of a serial monogamist. I've had a few serious relationships, but the ones I had lasted many years. My last relationship was with a woman named Angela. We were together almost twenty years before..." Danika's voice trailed off.

"Before what? Finn asked.

"Before she died of breast cancer." There. She said it, against Natalie's advice. It was bound to come out sooner or later.

"Both your dad and your partner died of cancer?" Finn asked, choking a bit on her bite of baguette, a strained tone in her voice.

"Yep." Danika looked down at the eggs that were just set. She slid the eggs out of the skillet onto a large plate. Then she shaved a bunch of truffle over the eggs. It smelled divine.

"Dinner's ready!" she exclaimed, placing a plate, utensils, and napkin in front of Finn who was staring at her with an odd expression Danika wasn't able to pinpoint. She got a weird vibe from Finn. Maybe she shared too much, went too deep. Natalie did tell her to keep things light and relaxed, and she'd blown it. *I'm an idiot,* she thought to herself. She scooped a heaping spoonful of the soft, velvety eggs and truffle onto Finn's dish and slid it across the center island to her. She made a plate for herself, poured them both more wine, and sat down next to Finn at the center island.

Finn leaned forward and inhaled the steam emanating from the dish in front of her. She picked up a forkful of eggs, asparagus, and truffle and ate it. The candlelight flickered as they both chewed in silence. "Now I understand why you wanted to make me eggs," determined Finn. "I totally get it."

Danika nodded. She would never look at scrambled eggs the same way again. "It's decadent." She took a sip of wine and looked at Finn. Their eyes met; Finn held Danika's gaze, making Danika feel famished in an entirely different way that would not be quenched with food. Finally, Finn broke their gaze by looking down at her plate.

Suddenly, the power kicked back on in a whirl of light and sound. Both of them jumped. It seemed as though a spell had been broken and they had both somehow returned back to reality before dessert had a chance to be served.

CHAPTER FIFTEEN

The following Monday morning after the incredible date and even more incredible kiss with Finn, the sun ascended over the horizon as if it was pulling off a light pink and yellow blanket. Steam rose from the pond, and off Danika's coffee mug as she took another sip of the nutty French Roast on a late July morning. After the severe thunderstorms of the past week, the oppressive humidity had given way to crisp, flawless days with bright sun and clear blue skies. It was a welcome change and respite from the overwhelming East Coast heat wave that had locked down the region for several weeks. Even the birds moved around with a renewed sense of energy and ease.

Danika leaned back on the sofa, her feet pulled up under her. She had things to do today, but nothing seemed to matter more than watching the sunrise and the world around her wake up. The truth was, she'd been awake for hours. She hadn't slept well lately, and she knew perfectly well that had a great deal to do with the elusive Finn.

She closed her eyes and thought again about Finn's kiss, which had quickly become one of her favorite pastimes, and indeed a new, ideal way to begin or end any day. The memory of their lips almost touching always sent a jolt of electricity right through Danika's body. Danika also sensed the energy left behind by their interaction. Even though it had been almost a week since that night during the intense thunderstorm where they shared more than eggs and wine, it was as if the memory had somehow worked its way into the very walls of the RV, emanating out like the scent from a candle.

Finn texted the next day to thank Danika for the evening and the food. The text was polite and succinct, like a thank-you note your mother tells you to send to someone who purchased Girl Scout cookies from you. Danika had responded with kind words of her own, hoping to see each other soon, perhaps go for a hike in nearby Tallman State Park, which overlooked the Hudson. But since then, Finn had not responded. Danika was hesitant to reach out again, not wanting to pester her. She couldn't understand the sudden chill from Finn after the kiss that rocked Danika's world.

Danika worked hard to keep her mind occupied with other thoughts. She stayed busy enough at home, preparing and fencing in a garden that she'd use next year for vegetables. She also finished setting up the new chicken coop by adding a series of features to ensure the chickens would be safe in this rural environment, and warm in winter. She installed wire under the coop and enclosure, wire over the windows and vents, and insulated the interior. She hired an electrician and purchased second-hand solar panels to light and power the coop for a small heater in winter. Her favorite feature was the solar-powered chicken door that automatically opened and closed at sunrise and sunset. All she needed was a few laying hens. Overall, she settled in quite well, and had begun to call it, and believe it to be, her home.

Today would be interesting. Danika was scheduled to spend time with Tony in the kitchen from ten o'clock to one, then she had the second installment of the weekly cooking class that evening at five. On the one hand, she was excited about spending time with Tony and his cooks in the kitchen tasting recipes and talking food. On the other, she was nervous about the evening's cooking class and wondered if Finn would show up or not.

Danika thought back to the uncertainty in her life a month or more ago and at how different she was then. Much had changed including the surroundings. She didn't merely feel like a different person, she knew she'd become a different person. The unsure, unsettled woman she once was seemed like a character in a book she once read that faded more and more out of view by the day.

She took a sip of coffee and heard a car's tires on the dirt road approaching. She peeked out the windows at a Prius pulling to a stop. She shook her head. Natalie was always an early-bird, but this was a little ridiculous. Stranger still that Suzie seemed to be with her, too. Danika looked over at the clock on the microwave. It was only six thirty in the morning. Danika rose and opened the door to her RV, watching Suzie and Natalie jabbering with one another as each hung their behinds out of the open door of the Prius's back seat. *What on earth are they doing?* Danika wondered, smiling at how funny her friends looked juxtaposed against the serene scene around them.

Natalie popped her head up and saw Danika watching them. "Hey! We didn't think you'd be up yet!" She yelled. In the next breath, she whispered to Suzie, who was only visible now by her flip-flops poking out of the back seat.

"What the hell are you two up to?" Danika asked, opening the screen door and stepping down from the RV.

"It's a surprise," Natalie yelled before poking her head back into the Prius.

Danika craned her neck to see in the back seat of their car. Suddenly, one very unhappy laying hen jumped out of the car and started running around, clucking and squawking. "Oh no!" Suzie cried, hopping out of the car. She was a tall, slender woman who perennially wore her long gray/blonde hair in a bun. In the next instant, at least five additional hens followed suit, acting just as distraught as the first. Natalie and Suzie ran in circles around the car trying desperately to catch the hens as they scattered in multiple directions, expressing their severe displeasure at the recent car trip.

"Goddammit!" Natalie swore, her hands up over her head in abject failure.

"I told you we should have boxed them up!" Suzie cried, running after one chicken with her hands outstretched.

The scene was so hilarious and unexpected that Danika had no choice but to put down her coffee mug on a riser stair to the RV to double over laughing.

"This isn't funny!" Suzie yelled. "Dammit, Nat. Tell her this isn't funny! How are we going to catch them all?" Six chickens ran in all directions, making a racket and taking in their new surroundings, but ultimately trying their best to steer clear of the crazy humans who brought them here.

"You brought me chickens?" Danika asked in between bouts of hysterics. "Chickens?"

"Yes, Einstein. We brought you chickens," Natalie responded.

"You didn't box them up before the ride?" Danika asked.

"No. My brilliant wife thought they would get carsick, so she let them roam freely in the back seat!" Suzie hollered, staring down Natalie.

"And did they get carsick?" Danika asked. She knew the answer, but she wanted to see the response.

"Yes! They crapped all over the backseat. There's bird shit everywhere back there, and it stinks like a barnyard!" Natalie screamed. God forbid anyone came between Natalie and her prized Prius.

At the mere suggestion of bird poop in the back of Natalie's car, Danika doubled over again in a fit of laughter. Her eyes teared up, and her stomach hurt. She finally had no choice but to sit down in the grass and suck in a few deep breaths.

"Oh, forget it," Suzie said in a defeated tone as she plopped down next to Danika. "They're yours now. You deal with them!" Natalie walked over and sat down on the other side of Danika.

"Man, you both stink," Danika remarked flatly.

"I hate you. Did I ever tell you that? We are no longer friends!" Natalie declared, staring at Suzie.

"What the hell are you looking at me for, this was your idea. I was only helping," Suzie opined.

"This wasn't my idea, babe. This was *your* idea. Remember? You saw the coop and said, 'Oh, wouldn't it be nice if Danika had hens? Wouldn't it be great if she had fresh eggs?' Remember that part, honey?"

"Yes, well, I may have said that, but I wasn't suggesting you go out at the ass crack of dawn and buy six of them with the bright idea of driving them over here before Danika woke up. That part was all you, *babe*," Suzie responded, poking her finger in the air in front of Danika.

"Whoever's idea it was, thank you. Not only is it possibly the most unusual gift I've ever received, but it was also the funniest, thanks to your standup comedy routine that accompanied the delivery. Honestly, I haven't laughed this hard in years." Danika put her arms around both of their shoulders and hugged them to her. You two should take this show on the road."

"Oh yeah, and what would we call it?" Suzie asked. "Eight Chicks and a Prius?"

"How about Poop, Poop, Prius?" Danika roared with laughter.

"You two are hysterical. I have no idea how you're going to get the chickens into their coop," Natalie said flatly.

"This is going to take all of us to herd them in the general direction. Don't think you're out of the woods yet," responded Danika. "They're already a little stressed. Let's be calm and work as a team to get them into the enclosure."

Natalie stood up. "Let's get this show on the road. I'm afraid we'll be running around all day."

"You mean like chickens with our heads cut off?" needled Suzie.

The three of them stood up and fanned out, walking and waving their arms slowly. They began pushing the chickens in the direction of the coop, which was about forty feet away, near the shed. The chickens seemed tired after their car ordeal, so moving them into the enclosure was less complicated than expected. It only took a few minutes to move them in. Once they entered the enclosure, Danika tossed a handful of grain for them to scratch around for and added water to the automatic fount.

"That was easier than I thought it would be," Natalie admitted.

Suzie looked around the coop and enclosure. "Wow. You did a great job with this."

"Thanks," Danika said proudly. "After a few weeks, they'll settle in, and I can begin teaching them how to be partially free-range, letting them roam when I'm around. This will keep them from getting bored."

"It takes that long?" Suzie asked.

"It can. It'll definitely take the chickens some time to get into the dawn and dusk routine with the automatic door, so they know how to get into the coop before nightfall. They'll catch on fast," explained Danika.

"Oh yeah, they've been vaccinated. The owner told me to tell you that," said Natalie. "And where did you learn about chickens? I thought your chicken knowledge was limited to making a great cutlet."

"I've been doing a lot of reading this week," admitted Danika.

"Right. Trying to keep your mind off the thunder-kiss?" Natalie goosed Danika in the ribs.

"Thunder-kiss? That's a little dramatic, isn't it?" Danika asked.

"You tell me. From the sound of it, it was pretty dramatic." Natalie made eye contact with her wife, who was giving her the eye as if to reprimand her for her tone.

"You're seeing her tonight in cooking class, right?" Suzie asked, much more gently than Natalie's ribbing.

"If she shows up, yes."

"What makes you think she won't go?" Suzie asked, fixing her bun.

"I'm not sure. Something definitely changed afterward. I mean, we had a great time and talked a lot after we ate, but it was like she pulled back and closed off. I can't explain it, except that I felt it," Danika awkwardly tried to explain to Natalie and Suzie.

"Maybe she wasn't prepared to feel what she felt," suggested Suzie in a soothing tone.

"Maybe. It feels like something else to me. I can't quite put my finger on it, but I know it's something more than that."

"I'm sure she'll tell you in her own time," Suzie concluded, but Danika wasn't as convinced.

CHAPTER SIXTEEN

"**B**ella! Bella! There you are. Ahh! I was afraid you would not show up because you thought I was crazy!" Tony bellowed as Danika tentatively stepped through the swinging kitchen doors at the Riverside Café grateful for the air conditioning on such a hot day. "Tell me. The *tartufi*, the truffles. What did you think?"

Danika smiled. "They were delicious but much more mellow than I expected."

"Yes. Yes. Summer truffles are always milder. Wait until November when we receive the white truffles from Le Marche. Those will blow your mind! Tell me, what did you make with the truffle?" Tony asked.

"Don't make fun of me; I'm not a chef. I made scrambled eggs!" Danika admitted sheepishly.

"Make fun of you? Why? That's my favorite way to eat summer truffle. Lightly scrambled, soft, velvety, the eggs are the perfect vehicle for the truffle. *Bene!*" Tony exclaimed loudly. "Come! Take an apron. We are working on our autumn menu. Sit down." Tony set Danika up on a stool across from the primary food prep area. Several other cooks, all men, were busy in the kitchen, each focused on their particular task. The cooks moved purposefully around the kitchen. The clank of dishes, the sound of chopping, cooking, stirring, all of it created a different atmosphere than the same kitchen possessed a week prior during the first cooking class. The bustle of organized activity mesmerized Danika.

Tony jolted her to attention. "Where are my manners?" Tony clapped several times and whistled. The cooks stopped working. "This is Danika. Her palate is gold. She'll be tasting with us every Monday." Tony pointed to an older man with a goatee who wore Mickey Mouse scrubs, bright blue Crocs, and a white cap. "That's Michael. We call him Cappie. He's been with me for twenty years, and I've only seen him without a cap on his head once."

"When was that?" Danika asked curiously.

"My wedding day," Cappie responded quickly. "I tried, but my wife told me the wedding was off if I wore it."

Danika smiled. Tony pointed to a younger man with a buzz cut, his brows furrowed in a severe expression. "That's Federico. He's been with us since graduating from the Italian Chef Academy in Rome last year. He is a genius with sauces. We call him Rico."

Federico bent over the stove stirring a large pot. He barely lifted his eyes away from the pan to Danika.

Finally, Tony pointed to a heavyset guy standing at the stove next to Rico. "And that's Jackie. A big old teddy bear of a guy who loves his Red Sox."

"Let me guess. You call him Sox?" Danika asked.

"Now you're catching on!" Tony smiled broadly causing Danika to wonder if he was ever grumpy.

"The four of you do all the cooking for the entire restaurant?" Danika asked incredulously.

"Yes, with the exception of two prep cooks, dishwashers, runners, and a part-time pastry chef, we do the majority of the cooking. Some restaurants have many line-cooks that suck the joy out of cooking dishes with love from start to finish. We're all connected, and we work as a team to create an entire dining experience for our guests," Tony explained.

"Oh. I had no idea how many people are needed to make a restaurant run," Danika stated.

"Our little restaurant employs twelve in the back of the house and ten in the front of the house," Tony said. "I like to keep it small and intimate for us, as well as for our guests. We are working on a few ideas for our autumn menu. Today, you're going to try four dishes, all fish for the entrees, and a light dessert. Next week, we'll focus on meat. Tony yelled, "Three out for soup."

The cooks yelled back in unison, "Yes, Chef!"

"We are going to start you with Ligurian mussel soup. Then, you will try prawn and porcini risotto, grouper matalotta-style, and finally Sbrisolona.

"I don't know what half of that means, but sounds good to me," Danika responded good-naturedly. She hardly believed her luck in getting this gig.

"I'll explain as we go," Tony said. Cappie positioned a steaming bowl of soup, laden with mussels and several slices of toasted bread, in front of Danika. Tony grabbed utensils and a cloth napkin setting them next to the bowl. He poured ice water into a tall tumbler from a pitcher on the counter. Danika placed her napkin in her lap and leaned over the steaming bowl. "Tell me everything as you experience it," Tony instructed. "Ligurian mussel soup is traditional. Simple ingredients cooked well."

Danika felt self-conscious as if she was about to begin an exam. "Well, the garlic punches me in the face."

"Too much?" Tony asked.

"Maybe. I'd be afraid to order this on date night, that's for sure." Danika used a small seafood fork to pull several mussels from their shells. She popped one into her mouth and started chewing, dropping the empty shells into a small plate next to the bowl. "The mussels are sweet and tender. Not chewy at all. I hate when mussels are overcooked because then it's like chewing a rubber band. It's hard to find the sweetness of the mussels, though. I have to work at it. The garlic is a little heavy. I like the fresh parsley. The broth is tasty. Is tomato in it?" Danika asked.

"Yes. Very little tomato paste," Cappie responded.

"Maybe a hint more? It might help balance the garlic, but the tomato flavor is so faint I can barely tell it's there. I do taste white wine. I'm not sure that cooked down completely." Cappie nodded and pulled out a small pad and pen from his breast pocket. He made several notes, nodding. "I added a little wine late. That's what you're tasting. I won't do that again!"

Tony took a spoon of the broth out of Danika's bowl. He tasted it carefully. "Yes, more tomato paste, but not too much that it muddies the color." Cappie nodded again, taking his own spoon to taste the broth as well.

Danika took a bite of the bread that had been soaking in the broth. "Well, I could eat seven loaves of this bread saturated in that broth, it's delicious. Do you bake the bread here?"

Tony shook his head. "No, we have it delivered daily from Arthur Avenue. Why bake it when we can get the best fresh?"

"Not to take away from this dish, but the bread is amazing." Danika continued to dip bread into the broth and eat. She wiped a dribble of broth off her chin.

"Anything you'd add?" Tony asked.

"Oh, I don't know. That's your area of expertise. Maybe a squeeze of lemon. It might cut through the garlic a bit and brighten it up a little more."

"That isn't traditional, but I certainly get your point." Cappie tossed Tony a half lemon. Tony quickly squeezed a bit into the broth. Danika took another mussel and a spoonful of broth. Tony did the same. Even Cappie walked over, grabbed a spoon and tried it. The three of them leaned over the bowl.

"I like the lemon," Danika said.

"Me too," commented Cappie.

Tony tilted his head. "Yes, this way, I agree. But next time when you add more tomato paste, we might not need it."

Cappie nodded in assent.

This is so freaking fun! Danika thought to herself as Cappie removed the bowl from in front of her. She took a sip of water. Before she re-adjusted herself in her seat, Rico placed a bowl of risotto with two big head-on prawns and arugula in front of her.

"This is prawn and porcini risotto, typical in Friuli or Venice. Made with Carnaroli rice with garlic..."

Danika took a bite of the risotto and continued, "onion, white wine, olive oil. A ton of butter because it's silky. Fishy without being too overpowering." She took another bite with the mushrooms. "The porcini adds a nice nutty, earthy flavor. I'm a big fan of porcini. Cognac?"

Tony smiled. "A touch."

"And I know you chefs are going to hate me for saying this, but I'm not a big fan of the whole prawn with the head on."

Rico scoffed.

"I get it. I know the head has all the flavor and it makes for a great presentation, but for the average diner, it's kind of intimidating, and off-putting. I probably would've tasted the prawn first, but the head scared me, so I stayed away from it. I'm sure you'll have some foodies who love the head on, but most average folks like me are grossed out by those black eyes staring back at us," Danika admitted.

Tony thought for a moment. "Rico, we can cook the prawns whole but de-head them for serving."

"We might need three prawns then. Two head-off will look too small for a dinner portion."

"That's true. Let's try it both ways later and see how that looks. I'm not sure we can adjust cost too much more. Sorry Danika, but if the margins don't work, the heads might stay on."

Danika nodded. Tony continued. "In the restaurant business, we try to keep to margins in thirds. That means one-third of the cost should be food cost, another one-third front of the house, and one-third profit. If we have to add another prawn, that affects our food cost, and if it goes over the margin, we lose money on the dish. Or, we increase the price, but then the question becomes will a patron pay an extra two dollars for rice?"

Danika never thought about how the pricing side of the restaurant even worked, but it made sense. She'd entered a whole new world and was loving the crash course education.

Next, Sox placed a beautiful square dish in front of her. "This is grouper, matalotta-style. Sicilian," he said.

This dish was right up Danika's alley. A colorful dish plated with red plum tomatoes, green zucchini, sliced ribbons of yellow bell pepper, sliced mushrooms and almonds, and anchored by the flaky white fish. She recognized a common theme of ingredients in the first three dishes. Garlic, olive oil, white wine, tomatoes, mushrooms, fish stock. "This is delicious. The fish is tender and light, but it stands up to the peppers."

Sox smiled broadly. "I like her!" he exclaimed. Tony nodded in assent. Danika leaned back for a moment, and Sox tried to take her plate away. She smacked his hand. "No way! Not yet," she chided him. "No way am I letting you take this before I finish it."

A few minutes later, Tony placed a slice of Sbrisolona in front of her with a cup of coffee. She patted her belly. She had better get on an exercise routine if she was going to keep this up long term. "Oh Tony, I'm stuffed!"

"That's because you ate everything!"

"What did you expect me to do? Taste the food and spit it out?"

Tony chuckled. "This is Sbrisolona. It's a traditional crunchy tart from Lombardia. It's simple but a clean end to the meal. I love it with a coffee."

Danika broke a piece off and popped it into her mouth. "Very crunchy. Like streusel topping. I can see why coffee or tea is perfect for it. It's almondy and buttery. Yum." Danika sipped her coffee. "Tony, how on earth am I going to cook with you later? I can't possibly eat again in like three hours."

Tony laughed. "There are worse problems to have."

"You can say that again," Danika said, laughing as she ate another piece of tart, trying to keep her mind from wandering back to Finn, and whether or not she'd see her later in cooking class.

CHAPTER SEVENTEEN

Four hours later, after a leisurely post-tasting nap back at her RV, Danika sat in the same seat inside the Riverside Café's kitchen nervously waiting for her other cooking class participants to arrive. She sipped a bottle of water and tried not to think about the butterflies fluttering around in her stomach at the mere thought of seeing Finn again. She knew she was acting like a teenager, fretting and worrying about a silly crush. Danika re-adjusted herself on the metal barstool. Even though she'd spent two hours in this very kitchen earlier in the day, she was excited to cook with Tony again. Some people paid thousands of dollars to attend culinary school to study with great chefs. She was not only learning from one, but she was quickly becoming friends with Tony and getting paid to eat his fantastic food to boot. She said a silent thank you for this new opportunity, realizing that she didn't express gratitude for all her life's blessings nearly enough. As more of her fellow classmates filed in, she silently decided to be more mindful to say thank you for the gift of her life.

Tony strode into the kitchen, tying a clean starched apron

around his slender waist. He winked sideways at Danika, which Danika assumed was his way of keeping their new arrangement between them. That was fine with Danika. She eyed the empty seat next to her and began to wonder if Finn would show at all. Tony placed single electric burners in the middle of each table, along with cutting boards, knives, and hotel pans full of various ingredients. Tony methodically walked down the line with his prep, but her mind was roaming elsewhere.

Then, Danika felt a light touch on her shoulder. She felt the heat flow from that spot on her shoulder down to her feet and knew instantly it was Finn. She leaned back to see Finn looking intently at her with those gleaming eyes. Danika's heart skipped a beat. She smiled.

"Hey. I wasn't sure if you'd come," she said quietly as Finn took her seat next to her.

"Why wouldn't I be here?" Finn asked, her eyebrows furrowed in question.

"I don't know. I thought maybe you had second thoughts after our, ah, date."

Finn tilted her head in confusion. "Why? What do you mean?"

Before Danika continued, Tony's booming voice filled the kitchen. "Okay class! Tonight, we are going to do work together on a two-course dinner. I opted to skip dessert today, to focus on two dishes. Our appetizer will be a white bean and rosemary crostini, and our main course will be an approachable dish for all of you, roasted chicken, potatoes, and vegetables. This is a one-dish meal you can easily make at home on a weeknight."

Several people in the class nodded in assent. Danika thought that Tony's voice and food descriptions had somehow turned her into a walking Pavlov experiment. The sound of his voice describing the dishes caused her stomach to growl in hunger.

Finn leaned over Danika, placing her hand on Danika's knee

out of sight from the others under the stainless-steel table. Danika jolted upright, causing Finn to smile mischievously. "I was going to tell you that I can hear your stomach growling," said Finn. Danika knew that her face had turned beet red. "Oh. Sorry. I really shouldn't be hungry, but Tony has a way of making me believe I haven't eaten in years."

Tony continued to talk in the background, handing out menu cards, cutting boards, knives and baskets of produce. Apparently, they would be working in pairs on their own dishes. Translation: Danika and Finn were paired, but Danika only heard that Charlie Brown teacher-sound *wa waa, waa, wa*. Her leg still tingled where Finn's hand rested moments ago. Danika knew Finn noticed her discomfort, and for a fleeting moment, Danika believed Finn to be enjoying it, and even attempting to heighten it.

"I think we're supposed to get cooking," Finn said, her lips turned up in a smile.

Danika re-focused. She had the distinct impression Finn cruised for a physical reaction. "Oh, right. Yeah. He said we would be working in pairs tonight."

Tony stepped in front of Danika holding up a bottle of white and red wine. "Which would you ladies prefer?" he asked.

"White" they both responded in unison. Tony nodded and poured two glasses of wine. "Now get to work!" he commanded.

"Yes, Chef!" Danika bellowed louder than she expected, causing Finn to laugh again. Great. She was making a total idiot out of herself. *Pull yourself together*, she thought.

Danika scanned the recipe card for the appetizer. It looked straightforward enough. "Shall we begin?" she asked Finn.

"Maybe you should do it, and I'll look on. I'm not very good in the kitchen," Finn said, taking a sip of her wine.

Danika looked at Finn sideways. "You're in a cooking class, for cripes sakes. This technically means you should learn to cook.

Here." Danika handed her two cloves of garlic. "Why don't you peel and slice these while I get started on the pancetta?"

Finn looked at the cloves of garlic with a blank look on her face.

"You don't know how to peel garlic?" Danika asked, surprised.

"No idea," Finn replied flatly.

"Let me get this straight—you bake, but you don't cook?"

"That's pretty much the gist of it," Finn replied.

"How have you survived all these years?" Danika asked, incredulous.

"Ever heard of takeout?" Finn shot back sarcastically.

"Wow. Okay. Let me show you. Everyone else is way ahead of us already." Danika took the flat part of the knife and laid it over the clove of garlic on the cutting board. With her other fist, she smashed down on the knife and clove. The pungent fragrance of garlic immediately burst forth. "Now you peel the paper, and you're left with the clove. Go ahead and pick up the knife."

Finn held the knife like it was a deadly weapon. "I'd really much rather drink my wine and watch you," Finn said, an imploring expression on her face that Danika promptly ignored.

"Keep the tip of the knife on the cutting board and rock back and forth on the center of the blade. You see how it slides to and fro?"

Danika showed her with her knife. Finn tried to do the same. She was able to do it, but very slowly. "Good," Danika said, "Right. Now make sure you keep your fingers tucked in over the food you're cutting. One slip and you'll cut your fingertips. You can let the side of the knife rest against your knuckles to protect your fingertips from getting cut. You see?" Danika showed her, but Finn still kept her fingers out. Danika showed Finn the proper way to hold the knife and cut by laying her hands over Finn's. At that moment, four hundred people could've screamed

"Fire," but Danika wouldn't have budged. She felt a trickle of sweat run from the base of her neck down the middle of her back. Finn sliced the garlic properly, albeit slowly. Danika felt her breathing. "Like this?" Finn whispered.

"Just like that," Danika replied. This did *not* sound like they were talking about slicing garlic. Danika's feet were numb. She cleared her throat and stepped back from Finn. Finn took a large gulp of wine while Danika quickly threw some olive oil into a skillet, turned on the electric burner, and expertly diced up a slab of pancetta in a few seconds. She tossed the pancetta into the pan, immediately causing the pancetta to sizzle. After lowering the heat, after all, she did not want to burn the pancetta —only render it —she tossed in the sliced garlic and a sprig of rosemary. Danika scanned the recipe card one more time as she sipped her wine. She didn't want to look over to Finn, but she felt Finn's eyes on her, and the sensation wasn't altogether unpleasant.

Danika stirred in the drained cannellini beans and squeezed a half a lemon into the pan, careful to squeeze it upside down, keeping the seeds in her hand, not in the pan. She lightly mashed the beans with the back of her spoon, careful to break them up without turning them to mush. Only when she completed most of the recipe did she glance over at Finn. "Why are you staring at me?" Danika asked as she stirred the beans and pancetta.

"This might be my new favorite pastime."

"Oh yeah, what's that?"

"Watching you cook," responded Finn without the slightest hesitation. "Quickly followed by my second favorite new pastime."

"Let me guess," interrupted Danika, as she sliced the rustic Italian bread on a bias.

"Eating what I watched you cook," Finn said with a husky edge to her voice that made a shiver run right through Danika's chest. She had no idea how she was supposed to focus on the rest of the class when she only thought of kissing Finn once more.

"What were you thinking then?" Finn asked, leaning in toward Danika.

"Um," Danika responded, blushing.

Finn took another sip of wine. "My sentiments exactly."

Danika looked at Finn earnestly. "So, you're not upset about last week, then?"

"I don't know why you keep saying that. I'm not upset. It was more intense than I expected. And, I mean, that kiss was..."

"Amazing," Danika said, her gaze squarely set on Finn's lips.

"No, that's not the right word." Finn scrunched up her face in thought. "Thunderous."

"Electric," said Danika smiling, a reference to the thunderstorm raging around them as they kissed that night.

"Exactly," Finn responded.

"How on earth am I supposed to concentrate on this dinner now?" Danika questioned.

Finn replied in a throaty tone, "I have an idea of what I want for dessert."

Danika's knees nearly buckled.

CHAPTER EIGHTEEN

T he long dirt road drive to Danika's RV on a hot and
incredibly humid evening felt like an empty stretch of
deserted highway in the middle of the night. Danika
gripped the steering wheel so tightly that her knuckles turned
white. She'd suggested Finn follow her in her own car, but Finn
had ignored her and climbed in the passenger seat next to
Danika. Danika tried to soothe her nerves by focusing on the
sound of her truck's tires spinning up the gravel road, but the
atoms of her body were wholly tuned to the woman sitting next to
her in the passenger seat, a mere few inches away. They did not
speak. The talking Danika wanted to do had nothing at all to do
with words but had everything to do with her mouth.

She tried to keep her mind from racing to all the uncertainty
about these new and intense feelings, and about her growing
anxiety over Finn seeing her naked. She thought about keeping
the lights off. Pitch dark might be better, but then she wouldn't be
able to see Finn and that, somehow, seemed much more important than her own flagging body confidence. Danika put the gear
into park and turned off the engine. She leaned back in her seat.

She had no idea what to say and found herself locked in compression while her mind raced. If someone told her four months ago that she would be sitting in a pickup truck in front of her new RV with a beautiful woman by her side that she desperately wanted to make love to—and the feelings seemed to be mutual—she would've laughed her ass off.

Danika must've chuckled out loud because Finn's voice shocked her back into her awkward reality. "What's funny?" Finn asked quietly, her voice barely above a whisper.

"This is unlike me."

"What is?" Finn pressed, turning to face Danika.

"All of this. The RV, this place, you here with me. That cooking class. If you had met me a few months ago," Danika paused and shook her head, looking for the right words. "I don't think the impression would have been memorable in a good way." Danika put the truck in park and turned off the engine.

Finn leaned closer. "I doubt that," she stated simply as if it was the most natural thing in the world to be sitting like this feeling what was passing unsaid between them while every nerve in Danika's body bucked and kicked. "Are you going to invite me inside?" Finn asked, in more of a statement tone than a question. Danika didn't look up to meet Finn's eyes that had turned dark like coffee in an instant. Danika cleared her throat and stared down at her hands.

"I didn't take you for someone this shy," said Finn as she rested her left hand on Danika's right knee. Every muscle in Danika's leg constricted. "It's been. A long time," stammered Danika.

"Let's go slow. Why don't we start by getting out of the truck? I think that's safe, don't you?" Finn asked as if coaxing a child off a ladder. Danika wasn't clear why Finn seemed so confident after her hesitation the other night. After all, they barely knew one another. Danika brooded in the dark. Finn had been less than communicative when it came to her own past. None of that seemed to matter, as if they had known each other all along but had simply lost touch for a while to take care of other things.

"Yes. Sure. Sorry," Danika said after a long pause and an even longer sigh. She opened the car door, causing the dome lights to turn on above them. Finn turned Danika's face toward her with her index finger on her jaw. "I don't know what it is about you, but I need to kiss you right now."

"I thought we were taking it slow?" Danika teased as Finn's lips covered hers with an intensity that Danika did not expect. At first, Danika's lips were frozen, as though Finn's kiss was intended to thaw out her petrified core. She felt Finn's full lips move, gently coaxing Danika into something other than submission, something more like persuading her to come in from the cold and sit by a warm fire. If Finn felt Danika's outright arctic apprehension, it didn't deter her in the slightest. Finn touched Danika's lips with the tip of her tongue, willing them to part. Danika relented mostly because she had no other choice. Danika felt a switch flip. Her mind stopped controlling the action or slowing it. Her body took over. That same body that hadn't taken over much of anything over the past few years was now hyper-aware, hyper-focused, and more prepared than Danika imagined. The funny thing was, her mind didn't stop; it shifted gears. Instead of hearing her own chiding voice rattle around the open spaces of her head, she felt connected to everything all at once. *How on earth could a kiss do that?*

Danika responded, and within moments, the kiss intensified further as their lips crushed together in a hungry, driving need for deeper connection. At that moment, Danika knew her lips had been created to kiss Finn's. It was magic. As Danika savored the kiss, she felt Finn's breathing quicken to match her own. A kiss like this was a beginning, a key that unlocked a door Danika had never known existed let alone passed through before now. It was an affirmation that the sum of her life and experiences over the past fifty-five years were mere practice, preparation for what was to come with Finn.

The only reason Danika broke the kiss was to jump out of the car to get inside as quickly as possible. Her internal gears shifted from first to fifth in a split second. Finn followed suit, running around the front of the pickup. They kissed again as if they'd been apart for months, years even. The hunger Danika felt deep within her was unlike anything she'd ever felt before, and it made every other kiss over the course of her life pale in comparison to this.

They half kissed half shuffled to the steps of the RV. "This is ridiculous," Danika panted. "Hold on a second." She fumbled with her keys to unlock the door and swung it open. Finn pushed her inside. With one hand on the back of Finn's head pulling her closer, Danika unsuccessfully felt around for the light switch with the other.

The swirled and rotated around the RV toward the narrow stairs to the bedroom. Finn mostly pushed Danika backward. Their eyes were locked on each other's, blazing with an intensity that came from somewhere far beyond the two of them.

Finn broke their kiss to quickly unbutton her jeans and drop them to the floor. As she stepped out of them, she unbuttoned Danika's khaki shorts and pushed them to the ground as well, revealing Danika's red Tomboy boy shorts. Finn backed Danika up to the edge of the bed and nudged her into a seated position. Danika obliged. Finn placed her knees on either side of Danika, straddling her. Danika's hands slid up and down Finn's muscular torso under her tee shirt over her arched back, cupping her ass over her black bikini underwear, sliding up her spine underneath the long single braid.

Finn quickly pulled Danika's tee shirt off, giving Danika no chance to object or worry about her body. She pulled Finn's off in response. Finn's back arched, pressing her torso harder against Danika's body, Finn's hands in Danika's hair, on either side of her face and neck as they kissed slowly, languidly, their tongues intertwined. Finn's tongue probing deeper with Danika allowed her all the access she wanted or needed. Danika moaned. Their heavy breathing filled up the bedroom like helium in a hot air balloon.

I love you, Danika wanted to say, to shout, to whisper in Finn's ear as she nibbled her earlobe. *I've waited for you my entire life*. The thought was replaced by the sensation of Finn's lips on hers, the dizzying feeling of skin on skin, of Finn's warm breath on her neck. Danika wrapped her arms tightly around Finn, wanting to hold her in place for all eternity. All of Danika's senses were overwhelmed by Finn, and she was aware of nothing else but Finn's body, her breathing, her very essence that expanded to fill up the room. As Danika pulled Finn closer, she wondered if the RV would hold them or if the fiberglass sides would just blow off.

Finn made Danika feel like the most beautiful woman in the world. Danika stopped worrying about her body being less than perfect. In Finn's arms, she felt flawless. Finn told her over and over again with her mouth and hands over every inch of her body, that she was enough, that she was magnificent, that she was made for Finn to love her this way.

Maybe it was because she was experiencing this as an older woman, perhaps it was because the passion was more than she ever thought possible between two people, but Danika found herself taken over body, mind, and soul by Finn. While Finn touched her, caressed her, moved her, Danika found herself thinking of the first moment their eyes met in the restaurant kitchen, the first instant she smelled Finn's scent of lavender and ocean. Her memory of their first kiss during the thunderstorm, the way Finn cocked her head to one side when she was curious about something. All of it flooded into her mind while Finn's body rocked and slid against hers.

Danika was conscious of fleeting thoughts like *this is where I want your fingers now* or *let me loosen your hair from the braid, so I can feel it fall around me.* Some voice deep within Danika told her that she should memorize every detail, every sensation as it occurred because it was essential to her very survival. Danika trembled and shook. *I loved you the moment I saw you,* she thought, her heart bursting. She was aware of Finn's tongue in her, her fingers, her scent, the sounds the made, and the way Finn's eyes shone in the dark watching Danika orgasm, the way their bodies molded and remolded over and under each other.

Somewhere along the line Danika left her own body behind and looked down at the two of them making love, blurring their own edges, transforming themselves into something new and different, something entirely unknown but all at once oddly familiar. How would she ever do anything ordinary again like drink a cup of coffee or tie a shoe without thinking of this? Nothing would be the same. *I am yours. I am yours. I am all yours,* Danika thought as she drifted to sleep against Finn.

CHAPTER NINETEEN

Off in the distance, Danika heard a bird chirping, then a guitar strumming. "Delicious Melancholy," one of her favorite songs by Tammany Hall, floated into her consciousness on a thin ribbon of sound. The mid-morning daylight nearly blinded her the moment she cracked her eyes open. She moved her hand next to her, where Finn had been, but felt nothing except cool sheets. She rolled over and looked around. Finn was nowhere to be found. For a split second, Danika panicked. *Was last night a dream? Had she imagined all of it? Did she fall asleep with music on?*

Then she heard the not-so-subtle clatter of someone banging pots and pans in the kitchen, and she felt her body relax. She stretched her arms over her head and pointed her toes. Her body was sore. Delectably sore, but alert and aroused. Shifting her body on the sheets sent a tingle down her stomach toward her crotch. She felt like a woman who had been properly loved for many hours. She had never experienced that sensation until now, sensing a quick pang of sadness at the realization just as pots and pans clanged again from the kitchen.

Danika rose and pulled on her red Tomboy shorts and a tee shirt. After a quick trip to the bathroom where she didn't even bother to look at herself in the mirror as she brushed her teeth, she padded barefoot down the few steps to the kitchen.

Aside from the fact that the kitchen looked like a bomb went off, her heart fluttered at the sight of Finn wearing nothing but a long tee shirt barely covering her bottom as she cooked breakfast.

Danika walked around the center island and tried to kiss Finn, but Finn pushed her away. "Don't. I need to concentrate. I'm making you breakfast. It was supposed to be breakfast in bed, but I'm sure this racket woke you up," Finn said firmly, with a hint of apology, her eyes focused on the stove.

Danika poured herself a cup of coffee and sat across from Finn at the island. It was unusual for Danika to watch someone else cook in her kitchen. She tried to think back to the last time someone had prepared anything for her. Natalie and Suzie did all the time, but that was different. Danika resisted the urge to jump in and save Finn from whatever she was intently focused on making. Instead, Danika leaned back in the high-top chair and sipped her coffee, amused at Finn's discomfort. To this point, Finn always seemed together and steady, so that watching her flail around the kitchen entertained Danika immensely.

"What are you making?" Danika asked innocently, but her mind was not on innocent things. It replayed moment after moment of the previous night in agonizing detail. She looked down at Finn's fingers and remembered how those fingers had handled her a mere few hours before. They made love on and off all night, and each time more intense than the one before it. *I can't wait to do it again*, Danika thought, smiling wickedly into her coffee cup.

"I can tell your mind is on dirty things," Finn said, jolting Danika back to the present.

Danika blushed. "How?" she asked, her eyes wide. "Are you reading my mind?"

"Babe, after last night, I'd say I can read all of you," Finn said, licking her lips, as she waved a whisk around in a circle, resulting in Danika's stomach doing another flip. They stared at each other for a long moment. Something sizzled and popped on the stovetop.

"Okay. Let's stay focused on breakfast, so we don't burn down my RV."

"Right. I'm making you my one and only specialty, and the one recipe my mother ever taught me before she was too drunk to stand up straight." Danika noted the hard edge to Finn's voice at the mere mention of her mother.

"Which is?"

"Frybread. It's Native American and actually has a pretty important place in Navajo culture."

"You're Navajo?" Danika asked, surprised.

"I am. Half Navajo. The bread can be savory or sweet. One of my favorite ways to eat it is with a hominy salsa, but I figured for breakfast, I'd do the sweet version which is dusted with cinnamon and sugar."

"And you said you didn't cook!" Danika exclaimed. "That hominy salsa sounds good. You'll have to make that one day."

"Let's save that for another time. I don't want to blow my entire repertoire in one swoop. I've never actually made this for someone else." Finn commented, checking the underside of the frybread as it bubbled in the hot oil, looking intensely at Danika as if making this recipe now had some deeper meaning.

"Why is this bread important to Navajo culture?" Danika asked, sincerely interested in learning more about Finn's background and culture.

"Oh, right, yes. Well, not for a good reason, really. Navajo frybread originated during the Trail of Tears. On the route, the staples of Navajo food like vegetables and beans weren't available. The U.S. government had no choice but to provide white flour, sugar, and lard to keep the Indians from starving on their way from Arizona to New Mexico. That's where frybread was born, and it's been made ever since as a reminder of what the Navajo people went through. Honestly, it's the only thing I really know about my heritage. Mom wasn't exactly maternal in that way, and I didn't exactly grow up on a reservation or anything." Finn placed a completed frybread onto paper towels and sprinkled them with cinnamon and sugar. She then dropped another spoonful of batter into the hot oil, causing it to sizzle again.

Danika observed Finn, noting a variety of emotions that seemed fleeting, but passing nonetheless across Finn's face. Finn's hair was not in a braid, but flowed freely, almost wildly around her shoulders and down her back.

"You didn't know your family on your mother's side? I mean, they didn't teach you anything?" Danika asked.

"No. I never met anyone on my mom's side of the family. They disowned my mother when she married my dad. They sent funeral flowers to the wedding and everything."

Danika's eyes widened. "Funeral flowers to a wedding? That's intense. Why would they do that? Because your dad wasn't Navajo?"

"Exactly. I love my dad, but he's as white as a person can be. He loved my mother, but her family never forgave her for marrying a white man, and she never really got over the pain of being shunned. That's why she drank. People think that kind of thing is in the past, but it's not. It still happens every day."

Danika stared down into her coffee cup. *Her family would hate me,* she thought to herself.

"What's going on in that head of yours," Finn asked as she flipped the frybread in the pan.

"Your family would hate me," admitted Danika.

Finn laughed. "Which part? Because you're a woman or because you're white?"

"Well, both, I guess."

"Nah. Don't worry about it. When I think of my family, I think of everyone on my dad's side, and trust me, they'd love you. I wouldn't know anyone on my mom's side of the family if I bumped into them on the street. It's a non-issue," Finn said flatly.

Danika rose from her seat and walked around the center island as Finn turned off the stove and placed the last frybread on paper towels. Danika took Finn's face in her hands and kissed her long and slow, feeling Finn's lips still swollen from last night's lovemaking.

"What was that for," Finn asked, a little breathless.

"Do I need a reason to kiss you?" Danika asked.

"You do."

"Because I wanted to," Danika replied, pecking Finn on the top of the nose.

"That's a good reason," said Finn.

They sat down across from one another at the small dining table. Danika looked out the window. It was a sunny, bright day outside. Only a few days earlier, she sat in this very spot looking outside, never realizing how strikingly different the same view would appear after experiencing what she did last night. It was as if she looked around without blinders on for the first time.

Finn placed a frybread on a plate in front of her along with a paper napkin. Danika smelled the spicy cinnamon as she took a bite. She chewed and swallowed, then took another bite.

"I take it you like it then?" Finn asked, appraising Danika's expression.

"I don't like it, I love it. It's not greasy at all. To say this bread is addictive is an understatement. It's like a churro, and a pizza had a baby." Danika washed down the last bite of her piece with a sip of hot coffee.

"You inhaled it."

"I did," Danika admit unabashedly, causing Finn to smile.

Danika looked at Finn and noticed the dark circles under Finn's ordinarily luminous eyes. Danika looked closer. Finn's complexion suddenly seemed flat, with a light-yellow tinge to it. Finn slumped in her chair, looking uncharacteristically dull. "Are you feeling okay?" Danika asked, concerned. "You don't look so hot right now."

Finn's voice wavered. "I think I'm exhausted. We didn't sleep much, as you might remember. Do you mind if I go lie down?"

"Not at all. Go right ahead. I'll clean up." Danika tried to keep the concern in her voice to a minimum.

Finn didn't even look at Danika or touch her as she passed by on her way back up to the bed. Danika sat back in her chair and picked at the frybread. If Danika didn't know better, Finn looked ill, and not the kind of sick that the flu brings, but something more serious, more sinister and threatening. It niggled in the back of her mind that she'd seen that look before, but she shut down that thinking immediately. Danika became so preoccupied and alarmed by the dullness she saw hiding behind Finn's eyes that she cleaned up the kitchen in record time before checking on Finn in the bedroom.

Finn was curled in the fetal position in bed, the covers up to her chin. Danika felt her forehead; it was hot and clammy. She sat down beside Finn watching her breathe, wondering what other mysteries about this beautiful woman had yet to be revealed.

CHAPTER TWENTY

Three hours later, Danika jolted awake after dreaming she fell from an airplane like a sack of potatoes. She sat upright the moment of impact. Her eyes opened and focused on the now familiar surroundings. As she regained consciousness, she wondered why she dreamed of falling, thinking that the falling wasn't terribly uncomfortable or frightening, as that dream had often manifested throughout her life. Before she tumbled too far down that particular rabbit hole of self-reflection, she remembered. *Finn!* Her arm involuntarily moved across the sheets to where Finn had slept for some time before Danika decided to lay next to her. Danika did not like the beginning of this habit—that of Finn leaving before she awoke.

At first, Danika only planned to spend some time near Finn to make sure she was okay, but as the moments passed, Danika became more relaxed and drowsy, even though questions about Finn's background and health circled round and round in Danika's mind. At some point, Danika also fell asleep. Now, Danika rose and stood near the bed, craning her head to the side to better ascertain Finn's presence in the RV, but heard nothing. In the silence, a worry crept in and began to occupy a corner of her mind that she'd recently worked hard to de-clutter.

After pouring herself a glass of water, she walked outside into the mid-afternoon sunshine. A light breeze blew the hair off the nape of her neck, cooling her down for a moment. Danika felt oddly overheated, overexerted, even though she'd only walked a few dozen steps since waking. She tented her right hand over her forehead and looked out to the pond. There, on the swim platform, she saw Finn lying on her back, completely naked, with her hands cradling her head against the wood. She had not yet seen Danika.

Danika thought about swimming out to Finn, but she decided against it. One thing she had learned over the years is that sometimes a person needed space. While Danika was aware of the cells in her body pulling her toward Finn, she resisted the urge to run out. Her younger self would have done that, the one who was always seeking out something from someone else. Now, Danika was older, wiser, and more understanding that space between two people was an essential component to being together. Plus, the image of Finn's body stretched out on her swim dock, with Finn's dark hair fanned out behind her, was more than enough for Danika. The July sun sparkled all around, and on, Finn, making Danika think she was looking up at the stars and not out in front of her. She'd never look at that view the same way again.

Danika sat down on the Adirondack chair and sipped her water. It was nearly impossible for her to keep her mind on something other than making love to Finn. She tipped her head back and closed her eyes, feeling the hot sun on her face. It was in that moment that it occurred to her she'd never had a real orgasm before Finn. She thought she had. It's not like she had many lovers over the years, but she'd had enough to assume she knew what she was doing. She inaccurately supposed she knew her own body and how it responded. Sex with Finn wasn't different, it was something entirely new. She'd never really felt her entire body give itself over to someone else before. She always held a piece of herself back either for self-protection or because she didn't know any better. But with Finn, she felt safe to let herself go because Finn was sturdy enough to catch her. That feeling of letting go and having someone catch her in return was unlike anything Danika ever felt with another person. Now that she knew better, she wanted to do it again, and again, and again.

A splash turned Danika's attention back to the present moment. She opened her eyes to see Finn swimming to her. Finn's body cutting through the water with precision. Danika smiled. Finn's name reminded her of a mermaid. She imagined Finn's lithe and tan body cut through the blue-green Malibu ocean as she paddled out on a surfboard. Some people were made for the mountains or the desert or the prairies. Finn was made for the water. Finn stepped out of the pond, water dripping down her body. She stared at Danika with a hungry expression.

"You're awake," she said, allowing Danika to openly stare at her body.

"I am now," Danika said, as she felt the heat rising from within her.

Finn smiled. "You're staring at me."

"Can you blame me?" Danika asked, as droplets of water slide down Finn's neck, down the space between her breasts to land in her belly button.

Finn pulled her tee shirt on over her wet body, causing the cotton material to stick to her curves. Danika wasn't sure what was more arousing: naked Finn or wet tee shirt Finn. She cleared her throat in an attempt to pull herself together.

"Are you feeling better?" Danika asked casually.

"Yes, much," replied Finn. "I think I was just tired." She quickly pulled on her panties, to Danika's chagrin.

"Maybe, but you didn't look tired, Finn. You looked sick, like something's wrong."

Finn turned herself sideways, twisted her hair, and squeezed it. "I'm fine," she said sharply.

Danika immediately caught the edge to Finn's voice. "Don't get defensive, Finn. I'm not judging, I'm worried about you."

Finn sat down on the other Adirondack chair. She looked out at the horizon. Danika did not press. The emotions moved across Finn's face, settled for a moment, then changed. It was as if Finn was processing what to say or how to say it, unable to grasp the right way to begin. "Finn, whatever it is, you can tell me. I wasn't born yesterday. I can tell something is up. I hope that whatever it is, you know you can trust me."

Finn looked at Danika was an expression that seemed sad to Danika. She lowered her head and stared at her hands. Danika leaned forward and placed her hand on top of Finn's and waited. After a few moments, Finn stood up. "You don't want me," she said plainly, her eyes somewhere else as if she was talking to a stranger. "I'm really nothing special." She turned and walked back toward the RV.

Danika resisted the urge to stand up and grab Finn, to follow her into what would undoubtedly be their first fight. She resisted the urge to hold Finn tightly against her, to whisper in her hair *I love you, nothing you'll ever say or do will change that.* Instead, she leaned back in the chair and looked out over the pond. An egret flew overhead; its slow and methodical wing beats helped to slow Danika's raging heart. After a few minutes, Danika heard a car approach on the gravel driveway. Finn emerged from the RV fully dressed, cell phone in her right hand. Without so much as a look in Danika's direction, she hopped into the Uber and slammed the door shut, leaving a trail of gravel dust in her wake and leaving Danika to tamp down her frustration and wonder if the walls Finn had up around her would ever crumble.

CHAPTER TWENTY-ONE

D anika passed through the next several weeks in a fog. July moved into August, bringing with it more cicadas and a deep, dark green to the foliage reminding Danika that fall was right around the corner. The New York nights began to cool, and the days began to shorten a few seconds here and there. She vaguely remembered little snippets of moments over the past few weeks like feeding the chickens, washing her truck, folding laundry on the bed where they'd made love. She attended three more cooking classes, but Finn hadn't shown up to any of them, and Danika had no recollection what recipes were even cooked. After the third tasting meeting at the Riverside Café, Tony sent her home. He said, "No, no. This will not do. You cannot taste food with a broken heart. It ruins the food. You're no good to me like this."

"I don't have a broken heart," Danika pleaded, trying to convince Tony as much as herself. "I'm fine."

"Tell your heart that," he responded, sending her on her way with half a key lime pie, a loaf of bread, and a bunch of ripe heirloom tomatoes.

Over the last few weeks, Danika exhausted every conceivable Google search about Finn. Most of the time, she came up empty. Finn had no social media footprint whatsoever, which made cyber-stalking a bit of a challenge, but she did learn a great deal about Finn's father. Finn had merely mentioned that edited movies, but she didn't accurately fill in the blanks. Those blanks were pretty big. Her father had won two Academy Awards for blockbuster movies. Finn grew up in an elite part of Malibu with celebrities like Barbra Streisand and Clint Eastwood as next-door neighbors. Wealthy was an understatement.

There was a story in a 2000 *Architectural Digest* that toured Finn's father's home. Apparently, her father was as good of an interior designer as he was a musician. He was handsome too, distinguished looking. The photos of him accepting the Academy Award showed a tall man with sharp features and a smile that matched Finn's.

All the information opened the door to more questions for Danika. Why was Finn here in New York when she had that kind of life in California? When Finn clearly loved the beach and surfing, why would she settle in a town along the dirty Hudson River? Where was Finn right now? What was Finn doing and who was she doing it with? Why would Finn walk away from what transpired between them?

Danika texted Finn twice over the past few weeks. She restrained from sending her text after text, to the best of her abilities. After the second text with no response, she tried to let Finn go, but space was the last thing Danika wanted. She'd had plenty of space over the years. She wanted Finn, and she wanted Finn to be next to her. Nothing else would do. But, Danika knew not to force the issue. Hours turned into days, and days turned into weeks. Soon it was more than a month since she last saw Finn. The image of Finn walked toward her, naked and wet, hadn't exactly faded into the recesses of her mind, nor did their moments together when they made love.

Now, as she lay in bed with the small windows of her RV bedroom open, she listened to the rhythmic sound of the cicadas and tried to piece together the meaning of the short time with Finn. None of it made much sense. One moment Finn was hot, the next, cold. After their first kiss, Finn had turned ice cold, followed by Finn driving the action the night they made love. It confused Danika because she preferred little drama and a straightforward approach. In the moments here on this bed with Finn, Danika believed she'd seen into Finn's soul, that they had shared something that had given meaning to their existence. For Danika, it was as if the earth had shifted off its axis, but apparently, for Finn, it was merely another night.

Danika didn't know what to do with the fragile ribbon of hope that floated in and around her insides. On the one hand, her rational mind told her to let Finn go and move on. Her ego was bruised. She worked hard not to feel angry or upset. People have one-night stands all the time. She knew she needed to pull up her big-girl pants, but it still hurt. Unfortunately, she seemed unable or unwilling to truly let go. She'd maybe go a few hours not thinking about Finn, but something always brought her mind back to the way Finn smelled or the way she cocked her head to one side when she listened intently. She tried to find meaning in her days without Finn but came up empty each and every time. No amount of heart-to-heart talks with Natalie helped ease her mind, and even Natalie who always had answers to everything was stumped by Finn's behavior.

The other part of Danika was more difficult to pin down. That was the part that screamed out for Finn in the quiet of a night like this. That was the part of her being she hadn't known existed until now. Even though all of the signs were pointing in one direction, something indescribable inside Danika told her that everything she felt was right, and real, and would be rewarded in due time. It was the *in due time* part Danika struggled with. How much longer should she wait? At fifty-five years old, she'd already waited a lifetime to fall in love for the first time in her life. Now, before things even got off the ground, Finn was gone, and Danika was left wondering what the hell had happened.

Space or no space, Danika needed closure. She had to understand why Finn abruptly pulled away. She needed to know once and for all if the tiny voice inside her was telling her the truth or lying. Finn's last words kept circling around Danika's head, bouncing around in the quiet hours of the night. "You don't want me. I'm nothing special," Finn had said as if she was a broken-down vehicle in a used car lot that Danika shouldn't waste her money on.

Suddenly, Danika sat up in bed. She had an idea, but it would have to wait until morning.

CHAPTER TWENTY-TWO

Danika paced outside the back of the Riverside Café as the sun peeked over the horizon. Her hair was disheveled, and she still wore her pajamas. She hadn't even bothered to put on a sports bra. Danika was well aware that Tony arrived very early to work on Fridays because of all the prep work before the busy weekend ahead. Sure enough, a few moments later, Tony pulled into the small lot behind the Riverside Café. He walked toward her carrying two cups of coffee.

"Here. This was for Cappie, but you look like hell and probably need it more than he will," Tony said as he studied the dark circles under her eyes and her overall less-than-together appearance. Danika smiled and gratefully accepted the coffee. She waited for Tony to unlock the back door of the restaurant and swing it open. She followed him inside as he turned on lights. Danika was grateful for a few moments alone with Tony before the others arrived.

"Un momento," he said as he disappeared into the dining room. Danika sipped her coffee, tasting the deep chocolate notes.

A few moments later, he returned carrying a slip of paper. "Here," he said simply as he sat down across from Danika at the stainless-steel counter. Danika looked down and saw an address. "It's Finn's. That's why you are here, is it not?" Tony placed his hand on Danika's shoulder like a brother comforting his younger sister.

"How did you know?" Danika asked, her eyes wide in surprise.

"Sweet Danika. You think no one sees what you see? You'd have to be blind not to notice that thing between you and Finn. It is special. It's worth fighting for. I wondered how long it would take for you to come here and ask me for this." Tony winked.

Danika blushed. "I thought of it last night," she admitted sheepishly.

"Well, what are you waiting for? Go find her."

"What if she wants nothing to do with me?" Danika asked, her voice wavering with uncertainty.

"If she ran from you, she's running from something much bigger. You'll calm her. You're stronger than you think."

Danika hugged Tony tightly until she heard him wheeze a little. "Not too tight, bella" he protested, smiling and hugging her back.

"Tell Cappie I owe him a coffee," Danika said as she ran out the door.

After plugging in the address on the sheet of paper into the truck's navigation system, Danika sat back in her car seat before shifting the truck into gear. What would she say to Finn? What if Finn didn't want to see her? Danika pushed all the uncertainty out of her mind as she drove in the direction of Finn's house.

Ten minutes later, Danika pulled off to the side of the road. She parked on River Road in Upper Nyack. The houses on one side of the street were mostly hidden, facing the Hudson River.

The houses on the opposite side were built up high on a hillside with spectacular views of their own. Danika looked around. Every house seemed like a multi-million-dollar compound with gates and flags and stone walls. This was not at all what she expected. She double checked the address on the sheet of paper. A perky woman with bleached blonde hair jogged past her, fake breasts bouncing in the early morning sunlight. This was definitely the right place. She wondered if she should turn back and go home, back to her RV that looked like a joke compared to these homes. No wonder Finn wanted nothing to do with her. Why would Finn want to hang out in her RV when she lived in a house like this? Danika's sweaty palms gripped the wheel. Suddenly, she suffered from a severe case of second thoughts about this plan. She glanced at herself in the rearview mirror and saw herself. Her hair was a mess. She wore pajamas that were too long and dragged on the ground. Her heart beat almost wildly in her chest. *This is not a good idea,* she thought to herself.

After a few minutes of repeatedly opening and closing her truck door, she slammed it once more and pressed the button for the ignition. No, she would not barge in on Finn like this. It wasn't fair, and it wasn't the right thing to do, and Lord knows her disheveled appearance wouldn't make a favorable impression. Finn needed to come to her when she was ready to talk. Pushing her before she was ready would only end in disaster. Danika checked her side view mirrors and slowly turned the car around, heading back to her little RV in the woods.

As she drove home, snaking her way southbound along the Hudson River, she thought about where she was with her life and why she'd pushed this hard with Finn. She rarely acted impulsively, forcing someone to be with her. Come to think of it, she never really had to fight for anyone. All of her lovers (not that there were many), Angela included, had always somehow organically morphed into relationships without her thinking too hard or trying too hard. And perhaps this was most telling of all: no other woman had ever walked away. Not like this. She'd never fallen for someone who didn't fall for her right back. Maybe that was the rub. Perhaps that was the thing that niggled at her most of all.

Danika stopped at a crosswalk and waited for several joggers to cross, bringing her mind back to the present. She had to do a better job of staying in the present moment. It wasn't useful to rethink the past or daydream about the future. She still had much to figure out. As she put her foot back on the accelerator and proceeded home, she tried to convince herself that if things were meant to be with Finn, something would change. Leaving all that up to Finn was the scariest part of all. At that moment, the lesson hit her like a ton of bricks across the face.

That was it. Danika had never given her heart over to someone else and trusted them to do right by her. She'd never really had faith. Up until now, Danika always kept a part of herself safe and protected. She'd been the dutiful partner, the caretaker on many levels, but she hid the most sensitive part of herself away as if Angela wasn't worthy of having her whole heart. As if Danika knew deep down Angela was not to be trusted or wouldn't know what to do with that most tender and vulnerable part of herself. With Finn, she'd given all of herself away almost immediately. She never made a grand announcement about this to Finn, but she felt her heart leave her on the night they made love.

She knew the exact moment it happened. They'd lain together after making love, both on their sides facing each other. Neither of them touched. Finn's hands were tucked underneath her head, and she stared at Danika in a way Danika had never been looked at before. Instead of looking away, Danika looked right back. Something transpired in that look between them.

Danika felt herself hand her heart over to Finn. She felt it leave her body and disappear inside Finn's chest. Now, wherever Finn was, she carried Danika's heart. The ache Danika felt in her chest came with the realization she might never get her heart back again.

CHAPTER TWENTY-THREE

"Something smells good," Natalie said the moment she closed the door to the RV on an unseasonably cool late September afternoon as the multi-colored leaves spun off the oak trees landing in piles around the pond and the RV. Danika stood in the compact kitchen frying chicken cutlets using her mother's recipe that she'd altered over the years. It felt like autumn, making her want to cook something warm and comforting.

Before Natalie arrived, Danika had decided to make her grandmother's favorite meal, something she referred to as Mimi's Sunday Chicken Dinner with herbed butter sauce. She took chicken breasts and sliced them in half, pounding them out until they were thin. She seasoned them with salt and pepper then moved onto the mixture of all-purpose flour with salt, pepper, and garlic powder. Then, Danika beat a few eggs and seasoned that mixture with the same and a pile of chopped parsley. Finally, she seasoned Panko breadcrumbs with lemon zest, Parmesan cheese, salt, and pepper. Satisfied her assembly line was ready, Danika heated canola oil in a frying pan and began the laborious process of flouring a chicken cutlet, then dipping it into the egg mixture, then finally coating well with the Panko before dropping it into the frying pan. She was careful not to over-crowd the pan or burn the breadcrumbs before the chicken cooked through. After about five minutes on each side, she removed the cutlets, placing them on a rack, to dry the oil on both sides. She seasoned each with a pinch of salt and a squeeze of lemon after removing the cutlets from the pan. Natalie was right, the RV smelled heavenly.

"Can you pull my sleeves up?" Danika asked as she continued her process, trying not to get her sleeves into the flour or egg.

"Sure, babe." Natalie came around the counter and carefully hiked up the sleeves to Danika's gray sweatshirt. She finished by giving her a kiss on the cheek. "You look like you lost more weight," Natalie said, eying the way Danika's jeans sagged around her hips and behind. Danika only shrugged in reply. Maybe she had. Maybe the jeans were too big. It didn't matter one way or the other, really. Natalie opened the refrigerator and pulled out a bottle of beer. She twisted the cap off and looked at the label. "Founders Mosaic Promise. Never tried this before. Is it good? I love the label." She pointed to the beer bottle label of a curvy woman with wavy red hair holding wheat in one arm and spilling a carafe of beer in the other hand.

"It is good. A little bit of a hop kick," Danika replied. "It's really a winter beer, but I've kind of been in a winter mood lately."

"Hmm," Natalie replied as she tasted the beer. "I like it. It's the kind of beer that warms you right up." Natalie looked over at the electric fireplace in the living area to the left. "You know that does look like a real fire. I don't know how they do it."

"I'm not sure it looks that realistic, but it does the trick. Where's Suzie? I thought she was coming too."

"She's home wheezing and hacking. She's had this cold for a week. I've relegated her to the guest room to keep her germs from spreading like wildfire. I told her if she didn't rest up, she'd be headed to the doctor. That was enough to scare her into submission. You know how much she loves doctors. I've never met anyone with more white-coat syndrome than my wife."

Danika chuckled. "Should we go outside? I have a fire ready to go."

"Nah. Let's eat first. I'm starving." Natalie picked up the remote and turned on the television. Her beloved Dallas Cowboys were playing the New York Giants. She pressed the mute button and returned to the center island.

Danika pulled the last cutlet out of the oil and seasoned it, setting aside the pan she fried the chicken in. Next, she moved onto her grandmother's famous herbed butter sauce. She melted butter in a medium saucepan and added a roughly chopped small garlic clove, sautéing for a minute or two before whisking in flour to form a roux. She tried to keep her mind on the mundane tasks of the recipe, knowing Natalie loved it. A pinch of salt. The zest from half a lemon. Cooking soothed her in a way nothing else ever did. When her mind was in a jumble, cooking helped to steady her.

Next, Danika pulled out a baking dish of mashed potatoes out of the oven along with a small cookie sheet of spinach-stuffed baby Portobello mushrooms. She'd no sooner closed the oven door before Natalie was at the center island, dish in hand, helping herself to the meal. "Honestly, I don't know what I love more, your stuffed mushrooms or those potatoes."

After both filled their plates, they sat down at the small dining table. Danika let Natalie have a seat facing the TV. "Cheers," Natalie said, clinking beer bottles with the less-than-enthusiastic Danika.

"Cheers," Danika replied, forcing a smile.

Natalie cut a piece of chicken and popped it in her mouth. She closed her eyes. "Oh my God. This is good." She peeked out the window in the general direction of the chicken coop. "I feel slightly guilty eating chicken with the chickens out there. How are they doing?"

Danika said nothing but raised her eyebrows. She looked at the chicken cutlet then back at Natalie. Natalie looked down at the piece of perfectly browned chicken on her fork.

"No way," Natalie replied, aghast.

Danika winked, then smiled.

"Jesus. You scared the crap out of me. I thought we were eating one of them."

Danika chuckled.

"Very funny. Here I think you're still Ms. Doldrums, and you play a dirty trick like that. You're not playing fair."

"Honestly, it's too easy with you. Like shooting fish in a barrel," Danika jested as the two ate.

"Yes!" Natalie shouted. "Dallas scored. Good." She took a moment to chew and swallow. "What've you been up to? I feel like I haven't talked to you in weeks."

"Not much is new. I haven't had much tasting to do with Tony the past couple of weeks, but he makes me come by anyway. I've been helping him with ordering and inventory while Mary is out on maternity leave," Danika explained in between bites.

"You're really learning the restaurant business. Maybe you'll open your own place. This should be on the menu," Natalie pointed down to her plate with the end of her knife.

"No, I don't think so. Restaurants are risky, and it's not like I'm a trained chef or anything."

"Funny you should mention that." Natalie leaned over to one side and pulled something out of the back pocket of her jeans. She placed a brochure for the Culinary Institute of America on the kitchen table. "It's right up Route 87 past Poughkeepsie," Natalie said.

"That's great. You thinking of attending culinary school? Danika asked wryly.

"Not for me. For you. It's only an hour or so away. You can take classes and still live here."

Danika shook her head from side to side.

"Why not? What else are you doing?"

Danika leaned back in her chair and placed her fork and knife down on her plate. "Nat, I don't need anything to do. I'm fine. I'm busy here."

"Doing what? Walking the chickens around the pond? Babe. It's me you're talking to here."

"What? It's not like I've been retired for long. It's only been like five months, no wait, less than five months. Give me a break," Danika said more defensively than she intended.

"I'm not saying you need to go right now, but think about it. It's not that I think you're lazy out here, it's that I think you need to get your mind off She Who Shall Not Be Named."

Danika's back straightened at the mere thought of Finn. After her near-visit to Finn's monster house almost a month ago, she'd tried really hard not to think about her, or say her name aloud, and that had become her full-time job. Some days she was more successful than others. She'd actually resigned herself to the fact that she'd think of Finn regularly here and there throughout the days and nights, and would always long for her.

Danika picked up the brochure scanning the headlines and photos while Natalie eyed her from across the table. "The thought has crossed my mind more than once," she admitted.

"I know," replied Natalie softly. "I'm worried about you. I love you, but you can't rattle around on this property all alone for the rest of your days. It's not healthy. And you love cooking."

"What if I fail out? I'm not exactly school material," Danika asked, an edge of uncertainty in her voice. She took a half-hearted bite of stuffed mushroom.

"This isn't like regular school. You know how to cook. You love it. It's hands-on. Big deal if you fail. You can do it for the love of cooking, not for the diploma. You can do it to learn and focus on something other than her. Expand your horizons, who cares what grade you get? It's not like you need to start a career or a life. You had a job. You have a life. Do this for you," Natalie almost pleaded.

"I don't know. I'd be pretending to be someone I'm not. Everyone there will be young and full of energy except for me, an old chubby chick who can't keep up."

"You know, I wish you would see yourself the way I see you. Or clearly the way Finn saw you."

Danika scoffed. "Are you kidding me? Isn't that the point? She saw the real me and ran as fast as possible in the other direction."

"Did it ever occur to you that maybe she's running from something else and what she felt for you was a little too big for her to handle? Sometimes people meet at the wrong time."

Danika looked out the window. "You know," her voice was barely above a whisper making Natalie lean forward to hear her, "that morning after we, you know..."

Natalie smirked. "You can say it. We're big girls."

Danika shot her a look. "After she made breakfast..."

"The Navajo frybread?" Natalie interjected.

"Right the frybread. We sat at the table, and Finn looked sick. I had a weird feeling."

"Like what?" Natalie asked.

"Like she had cancer. She had the same empty look in her eyes Angela had towards the end." Danika shook her head. "I can't explain it. I'm probably imagining things." Danika stabbed the placemat with the tines of her fork.

Natalie took a long look at her friend. "You might be imagining things. Maybe you were feeling guilty that you moved on to someone other than Angela?"

"Maybe," Danika replied, not convinced by her friend's suggestion.

The two finished their Sunday dinner in relative silence with Danika lost in her own thoughts as Natalie took turns watching the game and Danika. After both ate their fill, Natalie spoke up, her voice jarring Danika out of her reverie. "What do you say we go sit by the fire pit?"

Danika jumped up, happy to change subjects and shift gears away from those unsettling thoughts about Finn's mystery illness. "Sounds great. Can you clean up in here while I get it going?"

"Sure," said Natalie as Danika stepped out of the RV into the cold late September afternoon wishing deep down to see Finn already seated by the fire.

CHAPTER TWENTY-FOUR

Early the next morning before daylight dawned on the horizon, Danika lay wide-awake in bed replaying her conversation with Natalie. This pre-dawn think-fest had become entirely too commonplace over the past few months. She missed her clueless, blissfully solid sleep. She regretted telling Natalie that Finn looked as though she had cancer. Danika had tossed and turned all night, reliving the awful memories of watching cancer suck the life out of Angela's body and soul. While Angela wasn't the love of her life, Danika did care for her immensely. She'd blocked out or stuffed away many of those terrible memories after Angela died. Caring for her father during his illness had been an entirely different battle, but the sum total left her feeling remarkably tired and worn out all this time later.

Danika stared up at the ceiling listening to the heater kick on. She wondered if Natalie's words were right, that this would be the sum of her life. Would she live out her days alone on this little piece of land that wasn't even hers? The urge to feel sorry for herself tugged at her insides, making them taut and brittle like a stiff muscle on a cold winter morning. The thought of attending culinary school floated around her mind. She imagined wearing a starched white apron around her waist and some tough French chef yelling at her because she didn't dice onions fast enough. What would be the point of that? She liked her quiet life. Quiet was fine. She tried to convince herself that this property was a healing balm to her heart and that she didn't need more than this.

Danika turned onto her side. The memory of her first kiss with Finn shoved its way past all her other thoughts, despite her best efforts to block it out. She closed her eyes and felt Finn's full lips touch hers. She knew they fit together perfectly. Their lips fit, their bodies fit, and somewhere much deeper down, their souls connected. Why did Finn run from that? Danika tried to turn the experience on its side. Rather than feel heartbreak and sadness, she attempted to be grateful for the moments shared with Finn because they had been real to her. In fact, meeting Finn might have saved her life. The moments shared with Finn were incredibly memorable, and she'd treasure them for the rest of her life. Even if the love had been one-sided, even supposing Finn never loved her back, Danika tried to focus on feeling blessed that in this lifetime, she experienced real, honest-to-goodness love.

She thought again about visiting Finn, but something about that didn't feel right either, nor did writing Finn a letter, or trying to call her on the phone. Nothing felt right because, in the end, Danika knew she had to wait for Finn to come to her. Whatever it was that kept Finn away, Danika had to respect it even if she didn't like it. Danika knew this and had reminded herself of this more than once over the last few months.

She forced her mind on other things, unwilling to wallow in bed all day thinking about Finn, as tempting as that might be. Later this morning, she planned to take a ride to the local hardware store to purchase a heater and a tarp for the chicken coop. The chickens preferred the temps inside the coop to be around fifty-five degrees, but temperatures at night had begun to drop quickly, and she was concerned about the wind coming from the north. The chickens settled in well after their unique arrival. They produced so many eggs that Danika had more than enough for herself as well as for Natalie and Suzie.

Danika grudgingly sat up in bed as if trying to muster the energy needed to start the day. She could've stayed in bed for another hour or two, but what was the point really? It wasn't like she was going to fall back to sleep. She stood up and stretched, wishing for a fleeting moment that she was the kind of woman who did morning yoga and drank fresh-juiced smoothies as she padded down to the kitchen for a strong coffee.

A few hours later, Danika pulled into a spot in front of the local Ace Hardware store. It was a windy and damp morning and felt raw as if wet snow might fall at any moment. She zipped her purple Polartec fleece up to her neck and rushed inside. Danika loved this place mainly because everyone was always helpful and friendly. It cost a little more to shop there, but she preferred it to the vast and impersonal Home Depot a few miles away. She browsed the aisles with her cart, picking up some antifreeze, tarp, the coop heater, and a couple of suet birdfeeders that she knew the birds would appreciate in the cold weather.

As she stood in the checkout line, she checked her cell phone. Her friend Pete texted her that he had something important to talk to her about. She wondered if it had something to do with Mike Dunham, the guy whose land she was living on after he'd moved to Denver. Her last two rent checks had gone uncashed, and several phone messages to him had gone unanswered. She wondered if something was wrong. Hopefully, Pete would have some answers for her.

Preoccupied thinking about Pete's message, Danika didn't notice Finn enter the hardware store. The sound of Finn's unmistakable low timbre voice sent a lightning bolt of energy through her spine, causing her to jolt upright and look around. She turned to her left and saw Finn standing at the entrance of the store asking the Ace employee where to find watch batteries.

"Excuse me, ma'am, can I help you?" the polite cashier asked Danika, who, in turn, stared hard at Finn.

"I'm sorry, no, I forgot I needed one other thing." Danika blushed and stepped out of line, careful not to give away her presence to Finn. Her heart raced in her chest as she tried desperately to calm down her breathing by taking long, slow deep breaths that only made her look like a fish out of water gasping for oxygen.

She wheeled her carriage around the back side of the aisle behind Finn and peeked around the corner. Finn's ordinarily long braided hair was missing. She wore a baggy black hat on her head with no dark hair peeking out whatsoever. When Finn turned sideways to examine more watch batteries on the rack, Danika got a good look at Finn's puffy and shiny face that lacked arched eyebrows. The dark circles under her eyes made her look almost look like a character in a horror film. Finn's appearance unsettled Danika so much that she had to grab onto to the carriage for support. She was right. Finn had cancer, and from the looks of it, was far into chemo and radiation treatments. She'd lost all her hair, and the medication caused Finn's face to puff up as if she were a chubby child.

This explained everything. Danika's instincts had been correct, although this knowledge didn't exactly make her feel any better. Actually, seeing Finn look like a hollowed-out version of her former self-made Danika physically nauseous. She left her carriage and ran to the public restroom in the back of the store, barely slamming the door closed behind her as she heaved up her oatmeal breakfast into the toilet. On her hands and knees, her hands draped over each side of the toilet bowl, Danika shook uncontrollably. *Finn. Cancer. Finn. Cancer*—the words flew around her mind and slammed into her chest and heart like a gunshot ricocheting off cement walls. As she knelt in the restroom, she struggled with two equally competing urges. First, she wanted desperately to run to Finn and hold her, pressing her lips to her temple, and whisper in her ear that she was there, she would take care of her. *I love you*, she thought. *It doesn't matter if you have cancer and die. I love you all the same.*

But that wasn't entirely true. It did matter that Finn had cancer. The thought of watching Finn die the way Angela had was too unbearable to fully comprehend. Second, Danika wanted to run. She desired to run away from this place as fast as her legs would take her, unable to rise from the cold tile bathroom floor. All this time, she wanted to know why Finn had disappeared. Cancer was why. Now that she knew, she wished she could take it all back. Knowing was worse. Seeing the sexy, strong Finn look weak and weary was unbearable. But more than that, Danika felt unable to endure the realization that she wasn't strong enough to handle a loved one's illness all over again, even for Finn.

After Danika's full body shakes subsided, she cleaned herself up and splashed cold water on her face. She returned to her cart, looking for Finn, but Finn was long gone. As Danika stood in the checkout line once again waiting for her turn, she felt relieved that Finn did not see her. And that was the unkindest cut of all.

CHAPTER TWENTY-FIVE

S till reeling from the visit to the hardware store, Danika sat inside the RV on the black leather couch in front of the electric fireplace sipping a steaming cup of chamomile tea. Rain fell outside, making any outside jobs impossible. Danika wasn't sure what to do with herself. She leaned back into the sumptuous leather and put her feet up on the coffee table. She wondered about Finn's actual diagnosis, thinking it might be anything from a tumor to breast cancer or worse. Chemotherapy was used to treat a variety of illnesses and levels of severity. It was impossible to know much for sure by merely looking at Finn.

As the cold rain slammed into the side windows of the RV, Danika thought about packing up and moving somewhere warm for the winter. That had always been part of the plan. She never intended to settle here forever. The urge to pick up and run away held incredible power and Danika knew full-well why she wanted to run away. She wasn't strong enough to go through this all over again, least of all with Finn.

Her cell phone vibrated on the coffee table. She leaned

forward to check the caller ID, then picked up. "Hey, Pete. How's it going? Sure. I'm home now. You're welcome to swing by. Okay. See you in a few."

Danika dropped the phone on the couch next to her and sighed. Pete was on his way over. She sipped her tea and tried to keep nausea from returning.

A few moments later, there was a knock on the door. "Come in" Danika yelled as she jumped up from the couch. Pete entered quickly, standing on the mat to keep the water contained. His presence immediately filled up space, making it suddenly feel small and slightly claustrophobic. "Hey, Dan!" He smiled broadly as he peeled off his jacket and hat. Danika hung both on the coat rack next to the door and hugged Pete tightly, immediately comforted by his soft flannel shirt and cedar scent. Pete hugged her back. "Wow. What was that for?" he asked.

"I missed you, that's all," Danika replied, quickly pulling back. "Want a cup of tea?" Danika asked.

"Sure," Pete replied as he untied his shoes and took them off. "Man, it's raw today. I'm getting like my dad. I can feel the weather in my bones, and I don't like it one bit. Summer flew by. How come no one ever asks 'Wow, March is here already?'"

Danika nodded as she busied herself making Pete's tea. "You got that right. What's up with you? How are Monica and the kids?"

Pete's whole face lit up at the mention of Monica and his kids. "They're great. Can you believe Michael turned nine? And Daisy started gymnastics. You should see her flipping around the balance beam like it's no big deal."

Danika handed Pete a steaming cup of tea. "Let's sit down by my roaring fire," she suggested, smiling. She placed a plate of chocolate chip and M&M cookies that she baked yesterday on the coffee table.

Pete put his tea down on the counter to rummage around the inside pockets of his jacket hanging on the coat rack. "I almost forgot!" he said as he pulled out a manila envelope folded in half and brought it with him to the living area.

Danika glanced curiously at the envelope. "What's that?" she asked.

"Well, aside from wanting to see you and catch up a little, I am here on official postal business," Pete said slowly.

"Official business?"

"Yeah. From Mike Dunham." Pete took a sip of his tea. "Or more like the estate of Mike Dunham."

"Pete, what are you talking about? Is everything okay with Mike? I told you he didn't cash my last two rent checks."

Pete's face drooped like a big basset hound. "That's the thing, Dan, something happened to him. His ex-wife called to tell me that Mike passed away. Apparently, he committed suicide in Denver. I had no idea he was depressed or sick or whatever. Neither did his ex-wife. It was all really sudden."

Danika sat forward, her hand flying to her face. "Oh no. That's awful." Danika unsuccessfully tried to contemplate the rationale behind taking one's own life. Bad news came too frequently lately.

"I've been beating myself up since I found out. Mike invited me to Denver a couple of months ago, but I couldn't get away with work and the kids. You know this is my busy time of year."

Danika nodded. Pete was such a hard worker. In addition to his full-time job at the post office, he delivered firewood and snowplowed driveways in winter. Right now, Pete was struggling to keep up with the firewood orders from customers preparing for the long winter months ahead.

"I can't help thinking he called out to me for help and I didn't answer." Pete's head sagged into his chest.

Danika reached out and touched Pete's arm. "You had no way of knowing anything was wrong."

"No, I guess not, but still. If I had only gone to visit, maybe Mike would've talked to me, and things would have been different." Pete stared vacantly at the electric flames in the fireplace. Danika patted his big square knee. Pete took a deep breath. "Anyway, that's why he never cashed your rent checks." Pete picked up the envelope and handed it to Danika. "This is for you."

"What is it?" Danika asked.

"Go ahead, open it."

Danika unlatched the metal clasp on the manila envelope. She pulled out a piece of paper and unfolded it. As she read it, her eyes widened. "It's a deed to this property?"

Pete nodded.

"I don't understand." Danika looked up at Pete, searching his bearded face for an answer.

"Mike left a detailed will. He deeded this property to you," explained Pete.

"Why would he do that? He never even met me in person." Danika said, her voice rising an octave in surprise.

"He knew a lot of people in town, and apparently folks told him how happy you were on the property. He loved this place, and I think he really appreciated how much you loved being here too. He wanted the land to go to someone who would care for it as much as he did."

"This is beyond generous. I'm in total shock," Danika said, staring at the deed. "I don't know what to say. I can't even thank him."

"Sure, you can. Let's think about it this winter. I'm sure we can come up with some way to memorialize him out here," Pete suggested as he munched a cookie.

"That's a great idea," Danika admitted. We'll have to come

up with something big, something worthy of his generosity, but I don't know much about him."

"Mike was a pretty simple guy. He loved being outdoors," said Pete, giving Danika an idea that she needed some time to think through.

CHAPTER TWENTY-SIX

The heavenly smell hit Danika the moment she swung open the thick metal door to the Riverside Café's kitchen. Cinnamon, sugar, butter. It enveloped her in a cloud of warmth and comfort—exactly what was needed on a day like this. It took Danika twenty extra minutes to get into town slogging through the snow. The snowplows tried their best to keep up, but at two inches an hour, with heavy winds blowing from the Northeast, Mother Nature was in charge, and the plowing would barely make a dent in the heavy snow that fell on this cold February morning.

Storms like this, common in New England winters, were dubbed Nor'easters because the wind blew hard from the North and East usually bringing with it cold temperatures and foul weather. This particular storm, named David, was the third in a string over the past two weeks had dumped a combined three feet of snow on the sleepy towns north of Manhattan along the Hudson River.

After the second storm, Danika was grateful for her foresight in purchasing the bigger pickup truck and snowplow kit, too.

Both had come in handy over the past weeks as she plowed out the gravel road to her RV, in addition to getting around the rough roads to town.

As a general rule, she hated February. Nothing good ever happened in February. The days were too short, sunlight became too elusive, and the damp, cold wind blew and blew, keeping everyone inside. Danika hated feeling cooped up in the RV and regularly looked for ways to get out, even if that meant braving bad roads and terrible weather. Little trips to the library or the local coffee shop kept her from feeling like a hermit.

"Ahh, bella! I didn't expect to see you today," Tony hugged her as she unzipped her parka and peeled off her hat and mittens. "But I am happy you are here. I baked cinnamon rolls."

"Hey, Tony. Yeah, I've been going stir-crazy at home and figured I might be moderately useful here. I smelled the cinnamon rolls from the parking lot. If I was having second thoughts about coming in, that sealed the deal."

Tony placed a hand-sized roll in front of her along with a small cup of espresso. "Can you believe another snow storm? All this snow isn't helping business. No one comes out in this weather but crazy people."

Danika took a bite of the roll, its sugary goodness exploding in her mouth, causing her to close her eyes and hold up an index finger in Tony's face as if to say, "Shh, don't talk now. I'm one of those crazy people, and I need to focus on tasting this." Only after she took a sip of espresso to wash down the bite did she lower her index finger, giving permission for their conversation to continue.

"What are we doing today?" she asked, sucking the sugar off her fingers rather than wiping them with a napkin.

"Not much. There's very little prep to do on days like this because we don't expect many customers. I've cleaned everything there is to clean," said Tony with a bored expression.

"Good, that means there's time for us to talk about my big idea," Danika replied.

"*Un momento,*" Tony said as he exited the swinging kitchen doors into the front of the house. While she waited, Danika polished off the rest of the cinnamon roll and espresso. A few moments later, Tony returned with a cappuccino. "Okay. I'm all ears," he said, taking a seat on the metal barstool next to her along the stainless-steel countertop.

"Remember I told you about the guy who deeded me the land where I'm currently living?"

"Yes, of course. The poor man who died, yes?"

Danika nodded. "I've been trying to think of a good way to honor his legacy for giving me that incredible gift. He really loved the place, and my friend Pete tells me the guy—his name was Michael Dunham—loved the outdoors. I thought about creating a summer camp for inner-city kids to come each summer and spend a weekend camping and fishing, you know, getting in touch with nature," explained Danika as Tony listened.

"That sounds like a wonderful way to honor his life. How can I help?" Tony asked.

"Well, I thought maybe you'd be willing to hold a fundraising dinner here at the Riverside Café to help me raise some startup money to get it off the ground. I have no idea what I'll need, but I want to set it up properly, you know, as a legal non-profit and all." Danika took a deep breath and continued, "I don't want you to feel obligated or anything. I know how busy you are, and I would totally understand if..."

"Bella, *statazit!* In Italian, that means to be quiet! Of course, we can do that. I'll talk it over with the crew, but I can't see any reason why we couldn't help. We can plan a Monday night in March, which should give you plenty of time to use the funds to set up something for the summer. Maybe a four-course prix-fixe menu. How does that sound?"

Danika rose from the barstool and hugged Tony. "It sounds amazing. Thank you! I'm excited about it. What should we do first?"

"Well, since you and I are snowed in, let's brainstorm the menu," Tony suggested. "I have some new ideas. I've wanted to partner food with essential oil cocktails. Recently, I met someone named Julez Weinberg who wrote a cocktail recipe book called *The Essential Mixologist*. She's fantastic and has this incredible gift of infusing edible essential oils into drinks, giving cocktails an entirely new spin, but also providing some added health benefits too. I've wanted to bring her in for a special event. I bet she'd be interested in helping us out.

"Tony, that sounds great!"

"It'll be a good test for us also. If this works, we might change up our cocktail menu and even begin to infuse essential oils into our menu items," Tony continued.

"If you think this Julez will do it, I'm totally on board," Danika said.

Three hours later, Tony and Danika not only had the outdoor campfire-inspired menu complete, but they also set a date and set up the MailChimp email blast that would go out to all of Tony's list plus Danika's friends, and Michael's friends and family. Pete was tasked with helping pull the list together of people who knew Michael. Everything quickly came together, helping to make Danika feel certain the event would be a huge success.

They ultimately decided on four courses that somehow used fire to roast or toast some of the ingredients, giving the nod to a camping theme with an Italian flair. Antipasto would be grilled Wellfleet oysters with a sweet pepper-herb mignonette. They settled on a pasta dish of ricotta gnudi with brown butter, and sage. Grilled lamb chop with caramelized fennel, and salsa Rossa would round out the main course. For the finale, they would set up small flaming platters table side for guests to make their own

S'mores with homemade graham crackers and marshmallows, and a decadent semi-sweet dark chocolate.

Since most of the main dishes paired better with wine, Tony texted Julez, asking her to plan three appetizer cocktails that centered on an outdoors, camping theme. Julez responded almost immediately that she'd give it some thought and would donate her time to mix drinks during the cocktail hour.

As she drove home through what felt like a wall of snow and ice, she wished again, like she had often done over the past months, that she had someone to share this excitement with. For the first time in a long time, Danika felt like she was actually doing something worthwhile. She didn't feel like she was wasting time or passing the time, she felt useful and engaged, excited and hopeful. Of course, Danika would tell Natalie and Suzie. They were, and always would be, her biggest cheerleaders, but she wanted to tell Finn about her idea, imagining in her mind how excited Finn would be for her.

Since seeing Finn in the Ace Hardware store in October, Danika had developed a new habit of checking the local obituaries each day. It was a gruesome habit, but she had to know each day that Finn hadn't yet succumbed to the disease. Knowing that Finn kept fighting was enough for her to plow through the day ahead and still maintain that tiny glimmer of hope that one day, things would be good between them.

CHAPTER TWENTY-SEVEN

March came in like a lion, making New York feel more like Alaska. Danika checked the weather in Alaska for kicks, only to learn that it was a whopping twenty degrees warmer in Anchorage, and they'd had about thirty inches less snow than New York this winter. This knowledge didn't make Danika feel any better.

She paced around the inside of the RV as the sun dipped below the horizon and the snow fell again. This was not a good day for snow since the fundraising dinner at the Riverside Café for the new Dunham Wilderness Camp was scheduled for this evening. Danika had obsessively checked the weather over the past two weeks, dismayed that once again, the weather reports were less than accurate. She silently wondered if paying meteorologists by their accuracy percentage would help much. She decided it would not.

As she walked back and forth in her RV, Danika fretted about many details that she'd checked and re-checked a dozen times or more. The one hundred and fifty dollars per person, four-course prix-fixe tasting menu would raise over eleven thousand dollars.

Tony refused to let Danika pay for food and staff cost, his team donating the entire evening.

Danika prepared a short speech to introduce the camp and her goals for it. She had photos blown up of Michael growing up hiking and fishing, camping and hunting hung around the restaurant. Excited to share her dream of the camp with the seventy-five guests in attendance, Danika still felt extremely nervous and on edge. Public speaking wasn't her forte, and as a general rule, Danika hated the limelight. She struggled to shove her fear aside. This evening, this camp, was far more significant than her immediate discomfort. Although she never met Michael Dunham, she felt a kinship with him, a connection forged by loving the same piece of land. Whatever inner demons Michael fought in his life, Danika hoped that now he felt at peace.

Danika took one final look at herself in the mirror. She didn't own many dressy clothes, usually avoiding them like the plague. Danika wore black slacks with a dark red cashmere v-neck sweater, a Christmas gift from Natalie and Suzie. Natalie insisted Danika go out and buy a dress coat and new shoes, so Danika had grudgingly obliged by spending some time at the Harriman outlets, where she purchased a camel Calvin Klein coat, and a beautiful matching scarf. She also splurged on a pair of black Sedgwick Kate Spade boots, and a matching bag. The result wasn't half bad. She'd kept up with regular haircuts and colors, adequately hiding the grays. Applying dark brown eyeliner, blush, and mascara made the look complete without seeming overdone.

She heard a beep outside and peeked out the window. Natalie and Suzie were there to pick her up. She turned off the lights and headed for the door.

"Please tell me the roads aren't bad," Danika said as she slammed the back door of the Prius shut.

"The roads are fine. If they weren't, we'd be taking your pick-up," Natalie replied calmly.

"Don't worry, it's going to be an incredible night. We are proud of you!" Suzie remarked as Natalie drove. "Are you nervous?"

Danika held out a shaky hand. "More than a little."

"You'll be great. Imagine everyone is naked when you give your speech. I always heard that helps with anxiety," Natalie chimed in.

"Somehow the idea of looking at a bunch of naked strangers isn't exactly comforting to me," Danika replied as she stared at the wet and heavy snow stick to the side window of the car. "I hope the snow doesn't keep people home." Danika said, a worried tone in her voice.

"Don't worry. Everyone will be there. Have faith," Natalie commanded.

Fifteen minutes later, they pulled into the reserved parking lot behind the restaurant. The guests would begin arriving in the next half an hour.

Danika walked Natalie and Suzie around to the front of the restaurant. She knew enough not to take them through the kitchen, which would be a hive of activity right about now. They entered the front of the house and immediately stopped in awe. Tony had done an incredible job decorating the restaurant, making it look more rustic than usual with spruce boughs and twinkling white lights. The Italian landscape artwork around the restaurant was replaced with the large format pictures of Michael at various points in his life and over the archway into the dining room hung a banner that read Dunham Wilderness Camp. Natalie looked around and held her hand over her heart. "Danika, this is incredible. What you're doing is wonderful. Think of the kids you'll introduce to nature this summer, all in Michael's honor." Natalie wiped tears from her eyes and hugged Danika, who also held back tears.

Tony popped into the dining room. "Well? What do you think?"

Danika ran to him and hugged him. "Tony, it's incredible. I can't tell you how grateful I am."

"Wait until you taste that gnudi. Then you'll really hug me! I've got to run. Break a leg out here!" He quickly disappeared into the kitchen.

"What do we do now?" Suzie asked, looking around the empty restaurant, smiling at a few servers.

"We wait. And pray everyone shows up in this foul weather," Danika said, with a distinct edge of worry in her voice.

Thirty minutes later, the restaurant buzzed with energy. No one stayed home. Every single person who purchased the ticket showed. Pete came with Monica, his parents, in-laws and siblings. He cried so hard when he entered the restaurant for the first time, Monica had to escort him into the coat room so he could compose himself. Danika was overwhelmed with the love and support that flowed from Michael's family. Michael's parents approached Danika during the cocktail hour with tears in their eyes.

A diminutive, plump woman with dark eyes, Rita Dunham, exuded a fierce personality that belied her appearance. Her husband Salvatore kept his arm protectively around her waist as if he was holding himself up, not her. "I know we have never met, but what you are doing for my son Michael is a miracle. You never knew him, but you captured his joy of nature and love of being outdoors," she said while she hugged Danika tightly.

"Please know you are welcome to visit the property anytime, all of you," responded Danika. "And I hope you can see the Camp in action this summer."

"We will certainly volunteer. My husband can teach the children how to fish, and I can help cook."

Salvatore continued, "We were devastated by Michael's choice to end his life, but you have found a way to give him part of his life back through this Camp, and we will be forever grateful to you. A parent should never bury their child, and we will live with that pain for the rest of our lives, but you have given us something of Michael's to hold onto. Thank you."

Danika knew they felt close to Michael once again as they looked at all his photos around the restaurant, recounting stories about when the photos were taken. Interestingly, and to Pete's relief, Michael's ex-wife didn't show, but Danika didn't expect her to. It was better this way. Michael's family was able to feel his presence without the stress of his ex-wife being present.

Natalie approached her with two glasses in her hands. "These cocktails are incredible! Have you tried one yet?"

Danika shook her head. Natalie handed her one of the glasses.

"This is called the Grassy Knoll. According to Julez, who is tending bar, it has tequila, sake, cucumber and lime juices, plus lemongrass simple syrup infused with lemongrass essential oil. The kicker is the chipotle powder."

Danika took a sip. "Wow, it's incredible."

"Who knew drinking cocktails was good for you? Julez told me this drink helps promote a healthy outlook. I had no idea! I had a difficult time picking this over her version of the margarita or the lavender lemonade gin fizz."

"You might need to try all three. Hell, I would if I didn't need to give a speech," Danika announced, taking another sip of the magical concoction.

"Everyone is raving about the cocktails. If you stopped the event here, it would still be a huge success," Natalie said.

"And to think we still have a whole menu to come from an Iron Chef!" Danika clinked glasses with Natalie and smiled. She saw Tony peek his head out of the kitchen, her signal that she should get everyone settled into their seats for dinner service.

As Danika began to shush everyone to start her speech, the front door of the restaurant opened, allowing a cold gush of air to burst forth into the restaurant. Danika turned her head to look, thinking the door had swung open on its own. There, in the doorway, stood Finn sporting a cropped haircut, only a bit longer than a crew cut. She looked thin, and her hairstyle drew attention to her incredible cheekbones. She wore tight black leather pants, high black boots with a black faux fur coat with a red scarf.

For a fleeting moment, Danika thought back to the time when she tried a haircut that short and Natalie had told her she looked like a Muppet. Finn definitely didn't look like a Muppet. She appeared incredibly radiant, and healthy. Her cheeks were flushed red, and her eyes held that natural lit-from-within shine that Danika had found irresistible when they first met. If Finn was trying to make an impression with her outfit, she did. More than a handful of people turned to watch her walk into the restaurant. *Finn was definitely not going for that girl-next-door look*, thought Danika. Danika couldn't take her eyes off Finn. She looked incredibly sexy. Danika felt her knees wobble, and at precisely that moment, Natalie put her arms around Danika, as if knowing that she needed to be steadied. Natalie whispered in Danika's ear, "I get it. I totally get it." She squeezed Danika around the waist and gave her a slight push in Finn's direction before letting go and moving away.

Danika stepped forward. Finn stepped forward. If Danika could have emptied the room at that moment, she would have. Danika heard none of the voices around her or the clinking of glasses, laughter or music. All of it disappeared the moment Finn walked into the Riverside Café. Finn smiled, breaking the spell, causing Danika to step forward again. *I want to hold you. To tell you I've missed you and I love you. To tell you that when you are near me, I'm home,* Danika thought as she stared at Finn. *Should I hug her? Should I kiss her? What do I do?* Danika thought to herself as Finn smiled at her. She hadn't expected Finn; there was no Finn Gerard on the reservation list.

"Do you have room for one more?" Finn asked almost shyly, with her hands at her sides, waiting for Danika to make her choice. Danika looked at Finn's face, and for a split second, she thought she saw doubt in Finn's eyes—doubt that Danika would welcome her back, doubt that Danika even wanted to see her.

Every thought in Danika's mind centered on being cool, but every cell in her body and heart screamed for Finn. *You came back, you came back to me,* Danika thought, her heart racing. But reality smacked Danika squarely in the face. *Wait a second. How dare Finn show up unannounced like this on the biggest night in her life. How selfish. How incredibly rude,* she thought. Suddenly, Danika became torn with the overwhelming desire to hold Finn and hit her. Danika became aware of more than few guests staring at the two of them. She felt herself blush. Danika stepped back away from Finn even though every atom in her being leaned toward Finn.

"What are you doing here?" Danika asked, trying desperately to control her shaking hands and voice.

Finn looked confused. "I came to see you. I read about what you were doing, and I was proud of you."

"You didn't think to call first, to text me, to actually have a conversation with me before showing up like this?" The anger rose in Danika's throat as she nearly spat out the words.

"I'm sorry. This was a mistake. A terrible mistake." Finn turned to go, but Danika grabbed her arm.

"Look, you're showing up like this is more than a shock. I can't deal with this, and you, all at once. I'm pissed at you for leaving the way you did. It's been months Finn, months. But now isn't the time or the place to talk about these things," Danika said, surprising herself at how clear-minded she suddenly felt. Confident, even.

"You hate me," Finn said flatly.

"Finn, I don't hate you, but I can't do this now. Not here. Not like this."

"I get it, I really do. I'm an idiot for showing up like this." Finn fled from the restaurant as if it was burning down, leaving Danika in the entryway trying to pull herself together in front of a room full of people.

While Danika wanted nothing more than to run out after Finn into the snow and kiss her, she had a room full of people waiting for her. She paused and tried desperately to steady her ragged breath. *Inhale. Exhale. Inhale. Exhale,* she thought. After a few moments, she felt better, steadier. Danika turned to face the restaurant. She picked up a glass and fork and clinked the fork to the glass, then took a deep breath, looking briefly to Natalie and Suzie for the steadiness she needed. "Ladies and gentlemen, please be seated. I'd like to say a few words about why we're all here tonight."

CHAPTER TWENTY-EIGHT

Well after midnight, snow continued to fall outside, blanketing the Riverside Café and the entire town in a cocoon of quiet. Danika took a sip of bourbon, immediately warmed by the liquid as it worked its way down her throat. Natalie and Suzie sat to Danika's right in the empty Riverside Café dining room sipping red wine. Pete sat to Danika's left, after sending Monica home with their parents. All of the servers had already gone home. The rest of them sat in exhausted and companionable silence after sharing an extraordinary night to help launch Camp Dunham. Danika basked in the glow of knowing that her life finally had a purpose beyond herself.

The kitchen door swung open. Tony entered the dining room carrying a platter of food, followed closely by Rico, Sox, and Cappie, each holding dishes and platters. They all looked dog-tired; their ordinarily clean and starched aprons and chef coats smeared with food. Tony grabbed plates and silverware from the server's station while Cappie poured red wine for the men. The kitchen team sat down around the table with the ladies and began to serve up leftovers for everyone, whether they asked for it or not.

Tony lifted his glass for a toast and everyone obliged by doing the same. He declared, "To Michael. May he finally rest in peace knowing that children will love his little piece of heaven for many years to come."

"To Michael," everyone said in unison, clinking their glasses in a toast as the soft white lights twinkled around them.

The men dug into their meal with ferocity while Danika, Natalie, and Suzie joined in with a bit less gusto, although Danika did make sure to take a couple more of Tony's heavenly gnudi. Danika took a bite of the herbed ricotta gnudi with toasted hazelnuts, brown butter, and marjoram.

"I told you this gnudi would be a big hit," Tony commented as Danika smiled after taking a bite. Danika nodded again in appreciation.

"So good," Suzie agreed.

"The evening was a great success, Tony. Thank you all for your hard work. I'm so grateful for your support," Danika said as she rose and hugged each of the men, surprising them with the outward gesture. She looked around the room with tears glimmering in the corners of her eyes, her heart bursting with love. "When my father died last year, I remember thinking that I had become an orphan. Now, as I look around, I see all of you here and realize that I am not alone. You are my family, and I'm grateful to have your love and support." But as Danika said those words, the pang of missing Finn cropped up and lodged like a ball in her throat.

"Of course you have a family," Natalie said, grabbing Danika's hand as she sat back down at the table. Danika squeezed Natalie's hand back, feeling the circle of love between Natalie, Suzie, and her.

"I heard you had a visitor before dinner," Tony said to Danika in between bites, momentarily breaking up the love-fest.

"How did you hear?" Danika asked, eying him suspiciously.

"Nothing happens in this restaurant that I do not know about." He took a sip of wine and smiled. "What happened?"

"Finn walked in looking all New York City-stylish, telling me she read all about the event and was proud of me." Danika unsuccessfully tried to sound nonchalant.

"She looked good," Natalie said, observing her friend cautiously. "You told me she was beautiful, but I wasn't prepared for those movie-star good looks, am I right?" Natalie looked at Suzie, who nodded in agreement, as did Pete, with a mouthful of pasta.

"She did look good," Danika admitted. "Healthy."

"And?" Tony said.

"No, and," Danika responded after taking another sip of bourbon. "I sent her home. How dare she show up here after how many months, claiming some kind of lover's privilege to show up and be all supportive? It's ridiculous."

Cappie, Rico, and Sox looked on while they ate as if watching a riveting television drama.

"But she showed up," Suzie said gently.

"She did," agreed Natalie.

"Guys, gimme a break, it's been like eight months," Danika tried to argue, but even she was losing steam in her own stubborn argument.

"You actually kicked her out?" Tony said incredulously, shaking his head slowly from side to side.

"Yup. She kicked her right out. Finn looked devastated," Pete recounted.

Danika shot Pete a look. "Kicked her out is a little strong. I told her we had a lot to talk about and this wasn't the time or the place. I might've said something snotty about her not bothering to text or call or talk to me all this time before showing up."

"You kicked her out." Natalie stared sadly into her empty wine glass which Sox quickly refilled.

"Let me get this straight," Cappie said in between mouthfuls. "This chick you fell in love with has been M.I.A. for the last eight months. She might've been sick with cancer or something seriously life-threatening, you're not one hundred percent sure. She shows up tonight at your big event looking like a hot movie star, and you turn into the ice queen and send her on her way with her tail between her legs. Did I get that right?" Cappie concluded, looking from person to person around the table.

"When you put it that way," Danika said, hanging her head in her hands.

"Honey, you've got to fix this. You tend to have..." Natalie began before being interrupted by Suzie.

"...a little bit of a stubborn streak," Suzie finished Natalie's sentence.

"I'll say," chimed Pete.

"Now is finally the time to show up at her door," Tony concluded.

Sox pulled the glass of bourbon out of Danika's hand. "Hey!" she said in protest.

Rico surprised everyone by quietly finding Danika's coat and bag, holding the jacket up for her to slide her arms into. "What are you waiting for?" Rico asked, his eyebrows raised in expectation as he stood next to her chair.

Danika looked around the table and stood up. The people she loved most were pushing her out into a snowstorm, away from their table. She felt partly annoyed and partly exhilarated at the idea of finally settling things with Finn. "Guys, this is all well and good, but Natalie picked me up. I don't have my truck."

Tony disappeared into the kitchen.

"Oh yeah!" Natalie quickly stood. "She's right! I drove her here. I'll take you." She looked at her watch. "It's pretty late."

"Nat, the roads are a mess. Your Prius doesn't stand a chance. And too late for what? Will I turn into a pumpkin or something?"

Tony tossed Danika her truck keys. "When I heard Finn showed, I asked our intrepid dishwashers, Mike and Steve, to run over to your place and pick up your truck."

"Yeah, thanks to that bright idea, we've got extra dishes to wash tonight," Cappie complained halfheartedly.

"My truck is here?" Danika asked, surprised at Tony's ridiculous attention to all details in the midst of a hectic night.

Tony winked.

"I'll drop you off and take your truck home. Tony, is it okay if I leave my Prius overnight in your lot? We'll get it out in the morning," Natalie asked.

"Sure, sure, of course," he agreed.

CHAPTER TWENTY-NINE

Ten minutes later, Danika drove her truck, with Natalie and Suzie, over to Finn's house about five miles away from downtown Piermont. The roads headed to the little village of Upper Nyack were horrible; Natalie's Prius never would've managed. Danika navigated the snow-covered streets to Finn's house while she tried to think about what to say to Finn, or how to say it. Natalie and Suzie were right, she did possess a stubborn streak. The last thing Danika wanted to do was turn Finn away, but her pride had gotten the best of her. She wasn't mad at Finn for being there. She was upset with Finn for not acknowledging what she'd done first. If they stood any chance, Danika had to be honest, but she also wanted to find a way to reconnect with Finn. After all, it'd been many months since they were last together and Danika still had many questions that needed answering first.

Finally, after what seemed like an interminable ride, Danika pulled up next to Finn's driveway. She shifted into park and sat back in the seat.

"If anything happens, text me, and we'll come right back and pick you up," Suzie said gently.

"Be honest with her, but try not to get all stubborn and argumentative," Natalie chimed in.

"I'm not argumentative," Danika scoffed.

"I rest my case," Natalie retorted

"Okay, okay. I get it." Danika sighed and stared out the window at the falling snow. "What if this goes terribly wrong?"

"It might. But remember, Finn came to you tonight. Clearly, she wants to make things right, too. Don't get caught up in the minutia and remember she's been going through some rough stuff so cut her a little slack. Give her space to explain her choices and see if you can find a way to forgive her. If you can't, you can't, but try," Natalie said.

Danika opened the car door and felt a rush of ice-cold wind slap her in the face. Natalie popped out of the passenger's seat, ran around the car, and hugged Danika before climbing up into the driver's seat. "Get in there before you freeze to death," Natalie commanded before slamming the truck's door in Danika's face.

Danika walked with difficulty up over the snow bank that had built up from the multiple passes of the snowplows on the main road in front of Finn's driveway. Because the deep snow covered her ankle-high boots, Danika felt the ice-cold snow melt around her ankles in a matter of seconds. She gingerly made her way to Finn's front porch by holding her cell phone flashlight pointed downward. Once on the front porch, she tapped her feet on the corner of the porch trying to shake off some of the snow. Danika mustered up the courage to ring the doorbell. She waited, not sure if she was shaking from the cold, or from the nervousness that seemed to rise like an ocean tide from within her. Danika tried to peek in one of the narrow windows on either side of the front door, but saw only darkness. Her confidence waning, she looked at her cell phone and considered texting Natalie. They'd only be about a mile away. She decided to give the doorbell one more try.

She shivered in the late night cold on Finn's doorstep trying to determine if Finn ignored her, slept through the noise, or wasn't home. *What if someone else is with her?* Danika panicked. She hadn't even considered the possibility that Finn might have another woman with her. She backed up away from the front door and turned to go back out into the snow moments before a light turned on in the foyer. The door swung open. Danika turned back to face a sleepy Finn wearing heavy flannel pajamas with little flying pigs all over them.

"Danika?" Finn asked, hugging herself to the cold.

"Um, hi," Danika replied.

"It's the middle of the night."

"And still snowing!" Danika tried to sound chipper."

"What are you doing here?" Finn asked in a curt tone.

"Can I come in? My feet are wet and freezing, and you'll catch pneumonia if you stand in the cold much longer."

Finn hesitated, then turned her body sideways to allow Danika to pass. Once Danika stood inside the large foyer, Finn clicked the door closed behind her.

"How did you know where I lived?" Finn asked, still standing with her arms clasped firmly over her chest.

"Oh, right. Tony. He gave me your address a while back," Danika tried to act nonchalant.

"A while back? How far back?"

"Um, about six months ago, I guess." Danika replied.

Finn stared at Danika. "And why didn't you come here six months ago?"

"Well, I did, actually. But I sat outside and didn't come any closer," admitted Danika.

"Why not?"

"Well, way to jump right into things." Danika took a deep breath to steady herself. "I figured whatever your reasons were for walking away, they were your reasons, and it wasn't up to me to push you to talk to me if you didn't want to, as much as I hated it."

Finn didn't respond. She stood like a sentinel in the foyer with her arms folded across her chest, which seemed flatter than Danika remembered. Since Finn hadn't answered, Danika judged Finn's response by her body language. *This wasn't going well,* Danika thought to herself as she shifted from one cold foot to the other.

"Look, it was really shocking to see you walk in the door tonight. I wasn't expecting it, and I'm really not great with surprises. Ask Natalie. She tried to throw me a surprise party on my twenty-first birthday that ended before it began because I burst into tears and ran from the room when everyone yelled 'Happy Birthday.'" Danika took another deep breath. Rambling wasn't becoming on her or anyone. "Finn, it's not that I didn't want to see you, but I think we have a lot to talk about first."

Finn looked down at her multi-colored knitted socks and stared at the ground for what seemed like an eternity to Danika. Finally, Finn asked, "Why don't you come in and have a cup of tea to warm up?"

Danika took off her wet boots and coat, following Finn inside. As Finn turned on a few lights, Danika looked around. No doubt a seventies contemporary that had been gutted, the kitchen and living area formed one huge space, with floor to ceiling windows along the side wall that faced east and the Hudson River. Danika mused that the sunrise views from those windows must be extraordinary. Danika politely walked around the space looking at the expensive art and sculptures scattered about as Finn busied herself making them both tea at the expansive white marble center island.

The walls looked to be painted in a very light gray. The dark mahogany-stained wide-plank hardwood floors set off the white crown moldings, kitchen cabinets, countertops, and subway tile backsplash. Everywhere Danika looked, she saw expensive, classic but modern, and exquisite taste. It was as if she'd walked into a mashup between Pottery Barn and Restoration Hardware.

Danika stopped in her tracks to admire an oil painting in the living room of a woman lying on her side, her hips barely covered by a sheet. The image mesmerized Danika because it was at once focused and unfocused, soft, and incredibly personal.

Finn looked up as she poured hot water over the tea infusers. "That's my favorite. It's by the artist Shirl Roccapriore. I saw it in Provincetown when I visited for the first time this past August and fell in love with it. It's called *Reclining Nude Three*." She did a few other reclining nudes in the series, but I loved this one most. By the way, you're right, I do love Provincetown."

"I don't know much about art, but I can see why you love it, and I told you Provincetown is spectacular."

"It doesn't matter, it's all about how the art makes you feel," Finn said.

Danika thought about the inexpensive, most likely mass-produced Home Goods art hanging on the walls of her RV and felt a pang of embarrassment. Finn had expensive taste in art. Actually, Finn had expensive taste in everything from the looks of it, down to the cashmere throw blanket over the no-doubt Ethan Allen white linen couch. Finn watched Danika look around the room as she made the tea.

"Why don't we sit down?" Finn asked as she carried their tea over to the coffee table. Before sitting down, she tapped the remote control for the propane fireplace, which immediately sparked to life, adding a warm orange glow to the room.

Danika sat down on the couch and sipped her tea. Finn did the same. The two sat in silence for a bit before both of them began to talk at exactly the same time, making them both chuckle as well.

"I'll start," Finn said. "I clearly have more explaining to do." She slid a coaster over to Danika's side of the coffee table before placing her own tea down on another coaster. Finn leaned back on the couch and put her feet up on the coffee table, crossing them as if she was about to watch a movie rather than have an awkward conversation.

Danika thought for a moment about the snowstorm raging outside and imagined being curled up against Finn's solid side, under that cashmere throw, staring at the flames in the fireplace as soft music played. It was all at once as if that exact moment had already happened, and would no doubt happen in the future that left Danika feeling an odd sense of déjà vu.

"First, I want to apologize," Finn said softly. "At the moment, I didn't know what else to do."

"Which part?" Danika asked coolly. "The part when you took off in an Uber after we made love, or the part where you didn't bother to respond to any of my texts or messages, or the part where you didn't think to reach out to me at all for the last eight months? Or how about the part where you tell me you live in a mansion?"

Finn's eyes widened, and her face seemed suddenly sad, causing Danika to immediately feel sorry for the way she'd laid things out. "All of it," Finn said.

"I'm not—I mean—I haven't been waiting or searching for an apology all this time, Finn. More than that, I want to know why. Why did you walk away like that? Was it something I said or did?" Danika paused and stared at the fire before continuing. This was hard, but she needed to say it all. "Finn, I thought that what we shared was something special. Really special. I'm too old to play games or beat around the bush. It's not like I've had all these lovers over the years, but I felt something different with you, something powerful, and unlike anything I've ever experienced with another person before. I guess I thought you felt that too, but clearly, I was wrong. Maybe we just come from two different worlds." Danika looked around again at the well-appointed room. "I mean, now that I see the way you live, I can tell that my little RV would be slumming it for you."

Finn shifted to get closer to Danika. She placed her hand on Danika's leg. "You weren't wrong. I felt it too." Finn's voice suddenly changed and turned firm. "And wait one second. Don't you dare pull the *I'm rich and you're poor* crap. I've had to deal with that all my life. Before I moved here, I lived in a tiny beach house with four other surfers. So, don't presume something about me based on how much money you think this house cost."

Danika hung her head low. She heard Finn's words, but the hesitancy she felt at their different backgrounds concerned her.

As if sensing Danika's trepidation, Finn softened again. She squeezed Danika's hand. "Danika, I love your RV and that amazing property. It's like this oasis of serenity. You have no idea how refreshing it is to see someone choose to live simply. You're self-sufficient and everything is within your means. It's really sensible and down-to-earth, and it makes you so much more appealing to me."

Danika once again felt the familiar heat from Finn's touch and closed her eyes for a moment to savor it like one enjoys the first bite of a perfectly grilled steak. God, she'd missed that feeling. She opened her eyes to see Finn staring back at her intently. "Then why?" Danika said. "Why did you walk away? We could've gone slow. I wasn't expecting us to jump into marriage or anything, but I did hope to spend time together and take things day-by-day. Was it our age difference? I mean fifteen years is a big gap."

"It has nothing to do with our age difference. Honestly, I

could care less how old you are as compared to me. Was it a problem for you?" Finn asked.

Danika shook her head. "No. I can't say your age bothers me, but I do understand what it's like to be forty rather than where I am now, and I worry we may be in different places."

Finn pulled back again and looked for a moment at the fire. She picked up her tea and sipped it as if stalling for a few moments to gather the strength to speak. Finn exhaled a long breath, inhaled, then continued. "We are in different places, but it has absolutely nothing to do with our respective ages." She sighed. "I don't know where to start."

"Start at the beginning," Danika replied simply. "Tell me the truth. I can handle it."

CHAPTER THIRTY

F inn stared into the fire, then blurted out, "I have cancer. Well, had cancer, but I guess that's not the beginning." She shifted uncomfortably on the couch before continuing. "I told you I lived in Malibu and loved it. That's true. I had a girlfriend there. We were engaged, in full-on wedding-planning mode. I felt a lump in my breast in the shower, and after a bunch of appointments and biopsies, learned I had multiple tumors in my left breast, putting me in Stage 3A. Cindy couldn't handle the idea of my being sick. She walked out after eight years of our relationship without so much as goodbye. Actually, she ran," Finn said sarcastically, taking a sip of her tea.

"I guess it was better to learn that about Cindy before we were married, but it was like everything hit me all at once. Anyway, I moved back into my dad's house for a while. My dad knows the head of Sloan Kettering's Breast Surgical Service. Since I had an advanced cancer with a relatively large tumor deemed to be HER2—which basically means the tumor had a protein that's important for cell growth—we had to move quickly.

My dad got me in to see Dr. Morrow immediately, forcing me to quickly move to be closer to treatments. I hated New York City and the idea of living in Manhattan or any of the boroughs. This area seemed like a decent trade-off. Close enough to the hospital, quieter, and near water."

Finn continued. "This house had gone on the market after a full renovation. My dad insisted on buying it, wanting me to be comfortable here. I let him do it hoping he would leave me be. Sometimes my dad can be a little smothering when he goes into caretaker mode. He promised to give me my space, even though he hated the idea of my being here all alone. But after breaking up with Cindy, I wanted to be alone, and I needed to focus on myself without feeling like a child under my dad's care."

Danika leaned back on the cushions of the sofa, holding her mug with both hands. She didn't want to speak or break Finn's concentration. She needed to hear the whole story, but all of this talk about treatments and doctors was eerily familiar, and unpleasant.

"Anyway, not to bog you down with details, but I had just settled in and started hormone therapies before chemo when I met you. I certainly wasn't looking to date or meet anyone, but I was immediately drawn to you." Finn looked earnestly at Danika, making Danika's stomach flip.

"On one hand, I didn't want to get involved with you, but on the other, I couldn't quite stay away. That night when we first kissed during the thunderstorm, you told me that your dad and partner Angela both died of cancer."

Danika nodded.

Finn continued. "Angela died of breast cancer. It was all too much for me. I mean, that kiss floored me, but when you told me about all you'd been through with them, I just wanted to run, and I hated myself for it. Honestly, the word 'cancer' makes my stomach turn. At that point, I was still in a weird denial phase that I was sick—really sick—and might actually die. So, I took off and didn't share any of this with you."

"This is all starting to make sense," Danika said slowly, reliving the moments after their kiss and the way Finn seemed to shut off her emotions in the dark of the RV that night. The same pit in her stomach returned that she'd felt during Angela's illness.

Finn nodded. "Then, I wasn't planning on returning to cooking class, but I had to see you again. I wanted to see you again. And all those feelings I felt when we kissed came rushing back. I wanted to be held, to forget for a while that I was sick, and you're amazing, and beautiful, and sexy. I stopped thinking of anything except wanting to be with you." Finn stopped for a moment, her face flushed. "I know I'm rambling."

"You're not rambling," Danika said, placing her hand on Finn's leg. "I'm glad you're finally telling me the truth, as awful as it is to hear."

"Well, after we made love, which by the way, was incredible in every possible way, I felt really sick. I knew you saw it by the way you were looking at me. You already started putting the pieces together. I never expected to sleep as long as I did, but when I woke up and swam out to that awesome swim platform in your pond, I made the decision not to put you through this all over again, and I couldn't handle it if you decided to walk away like Cindy did, so I ran first."

Danika nodded. "Something about the way you looked reminded me of how Angela looked when she got really sick, and it did scare me. You should have told me, so we could talk it over rather than making the decision for me."

Finn continued, "You're right, but I don't think I was in the right frame of mind to have a conversation like that. Everything was all jumbled up in my head. I didn't see anything clearly.

Everything in my life had turned into worst-case scenario. I was forty years old and alone, without the person I thought I'd spend the rest of my life with, dealing with cancer from the beaches of Malibu. I met you not being ready for another serious relationship. Plus, the months after that weren't pretty. A double mastectomy followed by chemo and radiation kicked my ass. I didn't want anyone to see me like that except the nurses who my dad paid to care for me. He stayed with me for a month during the worst of it."

"I saw you, you know," Danika blurted out.

"You did? When"

"Sometime back in September. You were in the hardware store looking for batteries," recounted Danika.

"Oh, right. I remember that day. My dad had just flown out. He had a deadline for a film he was editing. I was so sick and had been cooped up for weeks. By then, I'd lost all my hair and felt like shit, but I forced myself out to do something normal." Finn paused and looked down at a leather watch on her left wrist. "When I started chemo, I became obsessed with time. I watched seconds pass thinking the sands in the hourglass of my life were shrinking by the moment. Not exactly positive self-talk. This was my grandfather's watch. He never took it off for as long as I knew him. After he died, my dad started wearing it. Anyway, I made my dad ship it to me. The watch stopped working, and I panicked that it somehow meant my life was over. I know, it makes no sense. That day, I was bound and determined to get a battery for that watch as if my life somehow depended on it."

"You looked really sick, and I knew you had cancer or something horrible."

"Why didn't you talk to me?" Finn asked.

"I was too busy puking in the bathroom. Seeing you like that terrified me. But it mostly scared me that I wasn't able to handle your illness. If you had told me, I wouldn't have been able to watch you go through that. Not after Angela and my dad. I was ashamed of my own weakness more than anything."

Finn nodded and sighed. "I know. I get it. I didn't want you to go through it either." Finn's voice changed, softened. "I made a promise to myself that if I got through the cancer, if I survived, I'd see if we could figure things out." Finn chuckled. "The Universe is nuts. The same day I received the test results from the doctor telling me I was one hundred percent cancer free, I read about your camp fundraiser in the paper. It was as if the two things were somehow tied together."

They both paused, as if digesting all the information in their own ways.

"You could've called, you know, rather than showing up tonight," Danika said in a slightly lecturing tone.

"What, you didn't like my entrance? I had it all planned," Finn remarked wryly.

"Your entrance was incredible. Those pants and boots," Danika whistled. "Let's just say you were the talk of the party."

Finn rolled her eyes.

Danika's tone turned serious for a moment. "And are you still cancer free?"

"After a double mastectomy, I am," Finn replied gently patting her flattened breasts.

"Boobs are overrated," Danika said quickly, causing them both to laugh out loud. Danika immediately felt relief, as if a giant balloon of stressful energy had been popped. "Thank you. Thank you for finally filling me in on all of this. The fact that you survived and are now cancer-free is truly remarkable." Danika scooted across the couch to be closer to Finn. She grabbed both of Finn's hands and held tight. Now that the past eight months finally made sense, all Danika wanted to do was hold Finn. "I'm sorry, too," Danika whispered, looking intently into Finn's once-more luminous brown eyes.

"What are you sorry for? I was the ass, not you."

"No, that's not true. Over these last months, I've really tried to look hard at myself and my shortcomings. I never really paid attention to that little voice in my head over the years, but we're finally starting to get to know one another. The thing is, Finn, you were right. I hate that you were right. I probably would've packed up the RV and taken off to New Mexico or something, and we never would have seen each other again. I have to apologize for being weak, but most of all, for not recognizing that in myself first."

"Can we shift gears for a second?" Finn asked.

"Sure."

"Obviously my timing is suspect, but I really am proud of you and what you decided to do with the Dunham Camp. Did he really commit suicide and leave you the property?" Finn asked.

"He did. It's still like a dream. No one in my life has ever done something like that for me, and here's this guy I never even met. I wanted to do something that would remember him in the best way possible, not focus on the way he died. Pete and I talked when he gave me the deed and mentioned something about how much Michael loved the outdoors. All of a sudden, I had this vision of little tents all lined up in front of the pond with inner-city kids splashing, playing, and running around in the open space. Tony and all the guys at the restaurant donated everything so one hundred percent of the proceeds would go directly to setting up the Camp. We hoped to raise around eleven thousand dollars but by the end of the night, several people donated more money and we ended up with almost twenty-thousand!" Danika recounted proudly.

"If you'll allow me, I'd also like to make a donation," Finn said, a warm tone to her voice.

"No, you don't have to do that," Danika said, slightly uncomfortable as she shifted on the couch.

"I want to. We'll talk about the details later. I'm proud of all you've done. It's really remarkable."

"But I haven't really done anything yet," Danika replied.

"You will. I know it. You're amazing," Finn said, her eyes full of love. She squeezed Danika's hands. Danika leaned forward and kissed Finn on the lips, surprising both of them. Danika couldn't help it. Now was not the time to be hesitant. Finn needed to know how she felt and she wasn't about to waste one more moment of precious time. Danika burrowed her face in Finn's neck, smelling lilac, smelling summer in her skin. She inhaled deeply. All her life, she'd wondered what it might be like to feel completely at home with another person. In this moment, Danika felt a homecoming like nothing she'd ever experienced before. Again, she thought, *I am yours. I am yours. I'll always be yours.*

When she finally pulled back, she saw that Finn had tears streaming down both cheeks. She placed her hands on either side of Finn's beautiful face and wiped the tears away with both thumbs. "Why are you crying?" Danika asked, suddenly worried that she'd gone too far too fast, here in the quiet of Finn's beautiful house.

"I thought..." Finn stammered, "you hated me. I was afraid to see you again after what I did."

"I don't hate you, Finn. Actually, I'm in love with you, and I think I have been since the first moment you walked into the Riverside Café's kitchen. My heart is yours no matter what happens in the future." There. She'd said it out loud to Finn. Maybe it was too soon to say this, but if there was one thing she'd learned watching people in her life struggle with cancer, it's that time was valuable. Every moment counted. She loved Finn and wanted to stop wasting time. After all, she'd be fifty-six years old soon and wasn't getting any younger. Time was a luxury for the young. She didn't want to waste another second wishing and wondering. Instead, Danika preferred to start living, and being honest with the woman she loved. Danika pressed on. She continued, "But I need to say one thing to you. And if I don't say it now, I'm afraid you'll never believe me."

"You could tell me that you landed on the moon last Tuesday and I'd probably believe you," Finn joked.

Danika squared her shoulders. "You need to know this. Whatever happens from this point forward, if you ever get sick with a cold or cancer, I won't leave you. Don't ever be afraid that I can't handle something. I might not handle it perfectly, but I promise to deal with it and not run away if you promise me something in return."

"What's that?" Finn asked.

"That you don't hide things from me. That you tell me everything, so we can figure it out together."

"That's fair," Finn replied without hesitation.

Danika smiled. No matter where the journey of her life might take her from this point forward, she would always have this moment to hold in the part of her heart that had never felt whole, until now. Finn had given her that gift, and she hoped to repay Finn over and over again for the rest of their lives.

"You know that painting you were looking at before?" Finn gestured to the reclining nude.

Danika nodded.

"I bought that painting because it reminded me of you. You looked like that the morning after we made love. Every time I look at it, I think of you and how much I love you."

Danika regarded the painting again. If only she were that thin. "You made me frybread."

"That's right, I did," Finn recalled, smiling. Finn looked

down at her grandfather's leather watch. "Wow, it's almost three in the morning."

"Right, it is late. I'll let you get some sleep," Danika tried to stand, but Finn held her hands down.

"You're not going anywhere," Finn said seductively causing a pang of something magical to ricochet off Danika's insides. "Plus, I'm not sleepy."

"Neither am I," Danika admitted as a blush worked its way up from her neck to her cheeks."

Finn laughed, apparently noticing the blush. She leaned forward and kissed Danika lightly on the lips. "What should we do now?" she asked innocently, her eyes flashing with desire.

Danika answered Finn's question with the kiss she'd been dreaming of for eight months. "I love you," she whispered against Finn's lips. "I'm yours, I'm yours forever."

Finn groaned as she hungrily kissed Danika back. Danika pushed Finn back against the couch, her hands sliding underneath Finn's cute flannel pajama tops. Finn froze with Danika's hand on her stomach.

"Don't," she said, pushing Danika's hand back down, her eyes filled with fear that made Danika's heart melt.

Danika didn't say a word. Instead, she slowly unbuttoned Finn's pajama shirt from the bottom up, with Finn's hand on hers, and their eyes locked. When done, she slowly opened Finn's top to see her once perfect and supple breasts gone, replaced by two lopsided, and still red, five-inch incision marks, cutting horizontally, and gruesomely, where each breast and nipple once was.

Danika looked up from Finn's chest to her face. She saw tears sliding down Finn's cheeks. "It's horrible, I know. I'm horrible and ugly. Please don't look." Finn tried to close her pajama top to cover the scars, but Danika held her top open.

"It's horrible, you're right. But you're not horrible and ugly.

Finn, you're beautiful. These scars are now a part of you, and we can work on healing them together." Danika knew the area around Finn's breasts would still be extremely sensitive and painful, so she bent her head down and very gently began kissing every inch of Finn's scars, from one side to the other. She felt Finn's body slowly began to relax into the sofa cushions. It didn't matter to her whether Finn had breasts or scars, whether her body was perfect or not. Danika only wanted to take away the pain of the last eight months, the pain of the treatments and the surgeries, the pain of cancer. She wanted to wipe the slate clean with her mouth and her hands, making sure Finn felt the same love and desire from her as before.

Danika heard Finn sigh as she kissed her way down Finn's stomach to the waistband of her pajama bottoms. She wanted to lose herself in Finn, in her scent, in her body, in her soul. Finn's hand in her hair told her she should continue, so she gently pulled down Finn's pajama bottoms, wanting so much to show Finn with her mouth how much she loved her, how much she wanted her, why she needed her.

In that moment, Danika understood the vastness of a love like this, the way it was capable of encircling any doubt or fear, any pain or heartache, any obstacle or barrier. As she tasted Finn and felt Finn's body rise up to meet her mouth, she finally understood that all her life she'd wanted to feel alive and in sync with her best self. She'd never known her best self until this moment, when she knew that the best part of herself belonged to the extraordinary woman underneath her.

A few hours later, Danika watched a reddish sun peek its way over the frozen horizon, creating rainbow-prismed icicles along the roofline of Finn's eastern-facing panoramic windows.

She looked down at Finn, who slept quietly next to her on the floor in front of the fire, her head propped up by throw pillows, her naked body covered by the plush cashmere blanket. Finn finally stirred, looking up at Danika. She lifted her head off the pillow and kissed Danika's shoulder. "Good morning," she said sleepily. "Now what?"

Danika kissed her back, running her hands through Finn's cropped hair. She tilted her head toward the incredible chef's kitchen. "Let's cook. Did I ever tell you I make a mean soufflé?" Danika asked, her eyes bright and hopeful.

The End.

EPILOGUE

Danika heard a knock on the RV door. She needed a moment to adjust to the surroundings of the RV, forgetting for a moment they'd been staying in the RV after spending the past few months at the newly renovated beach home in Malibu, where Finn ran her surfing school. Danika was so proud of the house they'd built there. It wasn't a massive mansion, but rather a fifteen-hundred-square-foot gorgeous, sustainable, pre-fabricated house made out of shipping containers. The house featured solar panels with battery backup that powered their entire house, a rainwater collection system, and a wastewater system used to fertilize and water their kick-ass vegetable garden. The one area they'd splurged on was the fully equipped outdoor chef's kitchen and dining area complete with a wood-fired pizza oven, where Danika spent most of her time cooking for friends and family. Finn's father loved Danika's cooking so much, he dined with them at least four nights a week and had recently been pressuring Danika to open a supper club. "Between these views and your cooking, who wouldn't want to eat here?" he said to her almost daily.

Danika stretched, smiling at the memory of Finn's father hugging her before they flew back to New York a couple of weeks ago. "My daughters," he'd said with tears in his eyes. "I always wanted two daughters." That acknowledgement had done something to Danika. It'd cleansed a part of herself to receive total acceptance by a parental figure after spending her entire life hiding from two parents who never could bring themselves to accept Danika for who she was. Finn had been right, of course. Her father did love Danika.

While it had been challenging to uproot herself to California, leaving New York behind, she learned to love Malibu the way Finn did. They'd developed a routine of sharing their lives between the things they both loved to do. Six months in New York, followed by six months in California. The best part of all was in sharing her life with Finn.

Hearing another, more insistent knock on the door, she jumped out of bed wearing only her old, ratty Melissa Etheridge tee shirt slash nightshirt, and ran to the door, swinging it open, rubbing the sleep from her eyes.

"Miss Russo? I think Curtis got stung by a bee." A young, gangly boy of about ten years old stood on the step of Danika's RV wearing only a ratty pair of boxer shorts and beat up Nike sneakers. The sun rose on the East, filtering a soft yellow light over the dozen dew-covered tents lined up on the side of the pond and the giant banner between the two Oak trees that read "Fifth Anniversary Dunham Wilderness Camp."

Danika looked from the boy to the other boy. The kid held his elbow with tears streaking down his face. She stepped out of the RV and checked out Curtis's arm. "No, honey, that's not a bee sting. I think you might've been bitten by a horsefly. Those buggers hurt, but it's not fatal." Curtis smiled weakly as Danika gave him a quick hug. Danika looked around. Pete snored loudly in the hammock near the pond and the children's tents.

"What are you boys doing up this early? Everyone else is still asleep."

"We wanted to go fishing. Mr. Dunham told us yesterday that the best times to fish are dawn and dusk."

"He's right. Give me a minute, and I'll be right out. We can try our luck on the East side of the pond, so we don't wake anyone else up. How does that sound?"

The two boys jumped up and down with glee, Curtis already forgetting about his bug bite.

Danika headed back to the bedroom to find a clean pair of shorts and a tee shirt. She stopped in her tracks mid-search to stare at the extraordinary woman lying in bed on her back, snoring softly, her shoulder-length black hair fanned out. Danika felt her heart expand with more love than she ever imagined herself capable of holding for any one person. She looked over at the silver wedding band on Finn's left hand. *Some honeymoon*, Danika thought, quickly dressing, throwing her hair up in a pony-tail, silently promising to make it up to Finn as soon as they were alone.

She moved into the bathroom to bush her teeth. As she brushed, she stared again at her reflection in the mirror. She recalled the time before Finn when she'd stared at herself in her parents' bathroom mirror wearing the same exact tee shirt. The self-loathing she'd felt back then, the sheer aversion to her life and her body, all flooded back to her. It felt like so long ago, as if an entirely different person inhabited the same, perfectly ratty and worn tee shirt.

As she wiped her face, a still very sleepy Finn came up behind her, wrapping her arms around Danika's thick torso and the tee shirt. She rested her chin on Danika's shoulder. "What are you doing up so early?" Finn asked, nuzzling her lips into Danika's neck, making Danika's head buzz with a slightly dizzy sensation that never seemed to fade no matter how long she'd been with Finn.

"I have two boys to take fishing for their first time," she said, leaning back into Finn for a moment before a busy day at camp began.

AFTERWORD

A breast self-examination (BSE) is a technique which allows an individual to examine breast tissue for any physical or visual changes. It is often used as an early detection method for breast cancer. Both men and women should perform a BSE at least once each month beginning at age 18.

Breast Self-Exam Tips

1. Do your BSE at the end of your monthly period.

2. If you are pregnant, no longer have periods or your period is irregular, choose a specific day each month.

3. This should not be performed in the shower or with lotion on your skin or fingers.

4. If you find a lump or notice other unusual changes, don't panic. See your doctor promptly for further evaluation.

For more information, visit the National Breast Cancer Foundation, Inc.

http://www.nationalbreastcancer.org/breast-self-exam

AFTERWORD

Author's Note

Food, and cooking it, has always played an important part of my life. Growing up in an Italian household, some of my first memories are of making fresh pasta with my grandmother. I was a lucky kid to have my maternal grandparents live across the street from me. I cooked often with them, making batches of all kinds of pastas including linguini and fettuccini, always laying the pasta on my grandparents' bed atop towels to dry. They taught me how to make Sunday sauce, how to seek out and admire fresh ingredients, and ultimately how to share food with those I love most.

I've always wanted to write a cookbook, and the opportunity to include recipes to this story presented itself early on. I didn't just want food to be described, I wanted the food, the cooking process, and the enjoyment of tasting that food with loved ones, all to be integral to the love story between Danika and Finn. Italians truly know how to show love through food, and I hope this book brought you, the reader, some of that love. I also hope you check out these recipes and try them for yourself. The recipes are in order of when they appear in the book.

Enjoy!

RECIPES

Recipes, unless otherwise noted, are the author's.

Danika's Cheese Soufflé: Serves 4

I've tried dozens of cheese soufflé recipes over the years. This one, is by far, the best, and most consistent. I've substituted Gruyére for cheddar, but the Gruyére is tastier! Recipe Courtesy Food & Wine http://www.foodandwine.com/recipes/best-ever-cheese-souffle

Ingredients:

- 1/4 cup plus 2 tablespoons freshly grated Parmigiano-Reggiano cheese
- 3 tablespoons unsalted butter
- 3 tablespoons all-purpose flour
- 1 1/4 cups heavy cream
- 4 large eggs, separated, plus 3 large egg whites
- 3 tablespoons dry sherry
- 6 ounces Gruyère cheese, shredded (2 packed cups)

- 2 tablespoons sour cream
- 1 1/4 teaspoons kosher salt
- 1 teaspoon Dijon mustard
- 1/2 teaspoon dry mustard
- 1/4 teaspoon cayenne pepper
- 1/4 teaspoon cream of tartar

How to Make It:

1. Preheat the oven to 375°. Butter a 1 1/2-quart soufflé dish and coat it with 2 tablespoons of the Parmigiano.
2. In a medium saucepan, melt the butter. Stir in the flour to make a paste. Gradually whisk in the cream and bring to a boil over moderate heat, whisking. Reduce the heat to low and cook, whisking, until very thick, 3 minutes. Transfer the base to a large bowl; let cool. Stir in the egg yolks, sherry, Gruyère, sour cream, salt, Dijon mustard, dry mustard, cayenne and the remaining 1/4 cup of Parmigiano.
3. Put the 7 egg whites in a large stainless-steel bowl. Add the cream of tartar. Using an electric mixer, beat the whites until firm peaks form. Fold one-third of the whites into the soufflé base to lighten it, then fold in the remaining whites until no streaks remain.
4. Scrape the mixture into the prepared dish. Run your thumb around the inside rim of the dish to wipe away any crumbs. Bake for about 35 minutes, until the soufflé is golden brown and puffed. Serve right away.

Beet Carpaccio with Arugula, Radish, and Grapefruit: Serves 4

This is a simple appetizer recipe that looks beautiful on the plate. The key is to source out local, fresh ingredients. Check out your local farmer's market. Recipe Courtesy of Food52.com
https://food52.com/recipes/20245-beet-carpaccio-with-arugula-radishes-and-grapefruit

Ingredients:

- 1 bunch of beets of your liking (usually 3-4)
- 18 oz. bag of arugula
- 10 radishes sliced thin
- 1 ruby red grapefruit
- 1 handful sugar snap peas

How to Make It:

1. Roast beets in 350-oven for 45 minutes or until done. Time depends on how large beets are. Cool beets.
2. While beets cool off, thinly slice radishes and slice the snap peas.
3. In a medium sized bowl zest grapefruit, next cut away peel and cut sections into bowl. Squeeze the juice from remaining grapefruit pulp into bowl.
4. Add sliced radishes to bowl. Toss with hands or wooden spoon.
5. Slice beets using mandolin or your incredible knife skills.
6. Placed sliced beets on serving dish. Sprinkle a few of the slice peas on top of sliced beets.
7. Add arugula to bowl with grapefruit and radishes. Toss.
8. Place on top of sliced beets. Sprinkle with sea salt or salt. Serve.

Squash Blossom Pizza: Serves 2

Squash blossoms are seasonal, and you'll only find them at specialty food stores or your local farmer's market. Don't wait to cook them. Buy and cook the same day. Or, do what I do and plant zucchini in pots just for the flowers. If you're not interested in making your own dough, you can always pick up fresh dough from your favorite pizza place or grocery store. Recipe Courtesy of Food52.com

https://food52.com/recipes/22416-squash-blossom-pizza

Ingredients:

- 1 round of fresh pizza dough at room temperature
- 8 squash blossoms, sliced in half lengthwise
- 1 bunch arugula
- ½ onion, sliced
- 1 small can of tomato sauce
- 1 cup parmesan cheese
- 1 tablespoon olive oil
- flour for pizza stone

How to Make It:

1. Place pizza stone in 450-degree oven for 1/2 an hour.
2. Roll out pizza dough and place on hot, floured pizza stone. Brush dough with tomato sauce. Sprinkle grated parmesan over sauce. Place sliced squash blossoms and onion on pizza. Lightly brush olive oil around edge of pizza dough.
3. Bake for about 12 - 15 minutes.

4. About 5 minutes before it's done, arrange arugula on top.

5. Remove from oven, cool for a few moments, cut and serve.

Cardamom Panna Cotta with Honeyed Figs: Serves 4

I don't know if there is anything sexier than fresh figs drizzled with honey. Fresh figs have a really short season, but trust me, they're worth the wait. This recipe just isn't the same unless you're using fresh figs and local, organic honey. Panna Cotta can be tricky. Definitely give yourself a test run before making this sexy dessert for your love. Recipe Courtesy of Bell'alimento

https://bellalimento.com/2013/07/24/cardamom-panna-cotta-with-honeyed-figs/

Ingredients:

- 2 cups heavy whipping cream
- 3/4 cup granulated sugar
- 1 teaspoon pure vanilla extract
- 1/8 teaspoon cardamom
- .25-ounce packet gelatin
- 3 tablespoons ice cold water
- 4 figs, quartered
- fresh honey

How to Make It:

1. Into a heavy bottom pan add: cream and sugar. Heat over medium heat whisking until well combined.

Allow to cook until bubbles start to form around the edges just prior to boiling.

2. WHILE the cream is cooking. Into a small ramekin add cold water and sprinkle gelatin packet on top. Set aside.

3. Remove from heat add vanilla extract, cardamom, and firm gelatin mixture. Whisk until well combined.

4. Equally divide mixture between 4 - 7.4 ounce-jars. Transfer to refrigerator to set up for a minimum of 2 hours.

5. Prior to serving, drizzle with honey and top with figs.

Burrata with Fresh Pesto and Baguette: Serves 4

Burrata cheese can be found at your local cheese shop or specialty grocery store. Be sure to eat fresh. If you can't, change out the water daily like you would with fresh mozzarella. I also strongly suggest spending a little more money on a good, extra virgin olive oil. I always recommend this for dishes uncooked dishes calling for olive oil.

Ingredients:

- 2 balls of fresh burrata cheese at room temperature
- 1 fresh baguette

For the Pesto:

- 2 cups packed fresh basil leaves
- 1/2 cup freshly grated Parmesan cheese
- 1/2 cup toasted pine nuts (optional)
- 3 garlic cloves (go lighter on the garlic if you want)
- 1/2 cup extra-virgin olive oil

How to Make it:

1. For the pesto, combine the basil leaves, Parmesan cheese, nuts, and garlic in a food processor fitted with the metal blade and pulse until the leaves are minced finely.
2. Add the olive oil and pulse to blend, stopping to scrape down the sides of the bowl.
3. Transfer the pesto to an airtight container and cover with a thin layer of olive oil to keep it from browning.
4. Let pesto sit at room temperature for an hour.
5. When you're ready to serve, drain burrata, pat try and place in a serving dish.
6. Gently break open the cheese and drizzle it with pesto.
7. Slice baguette in ½ inch rounds on a bias.
8. Scoop cheese and pesto on a round and serve.

Soft Scrambled Eggs with Asparagus and Summer Truffle: Serves 2

Summer truffle can be hard to find. I've ordered in the past from Urbani Truffles at www.urbani.com. The key to this dish is to cook the eggs very slowly over low heat, and to resist the temptation to overcook the eggs. I'm a big fan of fresh eggs that you find at your local farm. There's something about fresh eggs, at room temperature, that really helps to make this dish sing.

Ingredients:

- 1 1/2 tablespoons unsalted butter, at room temperature

- 4 extra-large eggs at room temperature
- 1/4 cup half-and-half or milk
- kosher salt and freshly ground black pepper
- 1 summer truffle
- 3-4 fresh asparagus stalks

How to Make It:

1. Place a medium sauté pan over low heat. Add butter and allow it to melt slowly.
2. In a bowl, whisk together the eggs, half-and-half, 1 teaspoon salt, and 1/2 teaspoon pepper until the yolks and whites are just blended.
3. Cut white ends of asparagus and dice stalks. Toss in pan and sauté on medium heat for a minute or two.
4. Pour the egg mixture into the pan over the asparagus but don't mix it.
5. Allow the eggs to warm slowly over low heat without stirring them. This may take 3 to 5 minutes. Be patient. COOK SLOWLY, over LOW HEAT. As soon as the eggs start to cook on the bottom, use a rubber spatula to scrape the bottom of the pan and fold the cooked eggs over the uncooked eggs. Be gentle. Once the eggs start to look a little custardy, stir with the spatula until they are the texture of very soft custard. Remove the pan from the heat before the eggs are fully cooked, as they will continue to cook in the warm pan.
6. Immediately slice the summer truffle with a truffle slicer or mandolin over the eggs.
7. Spoon the scrambled eggs into a plate and serve hot.

Ligurian Mussel Soup: Serves 2

I love mussels and have always found the best part of this simple, fresh dish, is dunking the bread into the soup! Be sure to visit your local fish store for fresh mussels. Recipe adapted from Academia Barilla.

http://www.academiabarilla.com/italian-recipes/ricette-liguria/ligurian-mussel-soup.aspx

Ingredients:

- 2 lb. mussels
- 2 cups water
- 1 clove of garlic
- 1 sprig parsley
- 4-5 tablespoons extra virgin olive oil
- 3 plum tomatoes, chopped
- 3/4 cup dry white wine
- Bread or baguette sliced and toasted
- 1 teaspoon salt
- ¼ teaspoon fresh ground pepper
- Grated zest of lemon
- 1 tablespoon lemon juice
- 1 small Vidalia or sweet onion, diced

How to Make It:

1. Place the mussels in the sink under running water. Pick up each mussel and check that it's firmly closed. Discard any mussels that are open or do not close when tapped. Scrub each mussel clean with a stiff

brush to get rid of any barnacles, pulling off the hairy 'beard' that sticks out from the shell, if it has one.

2. In a large pot, oil over moderately low heat. Add the onion, garlic, and lemon zest. Cook, covered, stirring occasionally, until the onions are soft, about five minutes.

3. Stir in the tomatoes and wine and simmer for 5 minutes.

4. Meanwhile, heat broiler. Put the bread slices on a baking sheet and brush both sides with olive oil tablespoons of oil. Broil the bread, turning once, until golden brown, about 4 minutes in all.

5. Add the water, salt, pepper, and mussels to the pot. Cover and bring to a boil. Cook, shaking the pot occasionally, just until the mussels open, 3 to 5 minutes.

6. Lay a slice of toasted bread in the individual soup dishes and pour on top the mussels and the stock. Sprinkle with chopped parsley. Discard any mussels that do not open before serving. Serve hot.

Prawn and Porcini Mushroom Risotto: Serves 4

Risotto is one of those dishes that requires your constant attention. Don't be put off by the steps involved in this recipe. You can always substitute shrimp for prawns, just be sure they are peeled and de-veined. Buying fresh seafood, rather than frozen, is highly recommended. Also, I highly recommend finding Carnaroli rice. It's called the King of Risotto rice for a reason. If you can't, use Arborio.

Ingredients:

- 2 lbs. large shrimp or prawns, peeled and deveined
- 1 teaspoon salt
- 1/4 teaspoon pepper
- 2 tablespoons olive oil
- 8 ounces porcini mushrooms, sliced
- 3 tablespoons butter
- 1 cup sweet onion, chopped
- 1 garlic clove, minced
- 1 1/2 cups Carnaroli or Arborio rice
- 6 cups chicken broth or fish broth.
- 1/2 cup dry white wine
- 1 cup frozen peas, small and thawed
- 1/2 cup parmesan cheese, finely shredded
- 1 tablespoon fresh parsley, chopped
- 1 teaspoon lemon zest

How to Make It:

1. In a sauté pan, heat 2 tablespoons of olive oil. Toss shrimp with 1/2 tsp salt and 1/8 tsp of pepper. Cook 3-4 minutes, stirring frequently.
2. Remove shrimp from pan and set aside.
3. Add mushrooms to pan and cook 4-5 minutes until browned.
4. Remove mushrooms from pan and set aside.
5. Add butter, onion, garlic, salt and pepper to pan and cook till tender 3-4 minutes.
6. In a separate pot bring, broth to a slow boil, remove from heat and cover with lid to keep hot.
7. Add rice to sauté pan and stir for 2-3 minutes.
8. Add wine to rice mixture, stirring constantly until wine is absorbed 2-3 minutes.

9. Add 1 cup of hot broth at a time, until almost all liquid is absorbed.

10. Every time the rice begins to look dry, add a ladle of hot stock and stir until the liquid is absorbed. Remember to stir frequently to keep rice from sticking to the bottom of the pan and making sure the rice always has some liquid to keep it from drying out. Rice should be tender, so continue this process for 25-30 minutes.

11. Add peas, shrimp and mushrooms to last 5 minutes of cooking.

12. Remove from heat and stir in cheese, sprinkle with parsley and lemon zest. Serve immediately.

Grouper Matalotta-Style: Serves 4

Matalotta-style is typical in regions of Sicily, Italy, known for using lean fish with a tomato-based sauce. You can easily substitute grouper with sea bass, haddock, perch, even trout. I love this dish with a fresh loaf of bread. Actually, I love pretty much every dish with fresh bread!

Ingredients:

- 2 lb. grouper fillets, wash, pat dry and cut into 4
- 2 tablespoons of olive oil
- 1 medium onion, sliced
- 2 cloves of sliced garlic crushed
- 4 fresh tomatoes or 1 ½ cups of canned peeled tomato
- ½ cup of white wine
- ½ cup of green olives pitted
- 2 tablespoons of capers

- ¼ cup of parsley leaves, finely chopped
- Salt and pepper to taste
- 1 bay leaf
- Parsley sprigs for garnish

How to Make It:

1. Rinse the tomatoes well. Peel off the skin, cut in half, remove some seeds and dice. If using canned tomatoes remove some seed and chop them coarsely. Sprinkle tomatoes with ¼ teaspoon of salt and set aside.
2. In a large skillet, over a medium heat combine onions and the oil, sauté for about 5 minutes, add the garlic and continue cooking until golden, total time 8 to 10 minutes. Remove and discard the garlic. (Keep the garlic if you want more garlic punch.)
3. Set on fish fillets on top of the sautéed onions along with the bay leaf, season with salt and pepper, moisten with the wine and increase the heat to high to evaporate the alcohol. Cook for about 1-2 minutes.
4. Cover the fillets with the parsley, chopped tomato, olives, and capers, add ½ cup of water, cover the skillet tight and let simmer at low heat for 15 to 20 minutes.
5. Transfer to a serving dish and spoon the cooking sauce on the top.
6. Garnish with parsley sprigs, serve hot.

Sbrisolona Dessert: Serves 4

I'm normally not a big lover of desserts, or of baking, but this recipe is simple and tasty. I find it light and not too sweet. Recipe Courtesy of Food52.com

https://food52.com/recipes/31863-sbrisolona

Ingredients:

- 1 ½ cups almonds
- 1 ½ cups all-purpose flour
- 1 cup semolina flour
- 1 cup granulated sugar
- ½ teaspoon kosher salt
- Grated zest of 1 large orange
- 1 teaspoon anise seed, plus more for top of cake
- 1 cup unsalted butter, softened
- 2 large egg yolks
- Powdered sugar, for dusting (optional)

How to Make It:

1. Preheat oven to 350 degrees. Grease a 10-inch springform pan or a tart pan with a removable bottom. Line with parchment and grease the parchment.
2. Reserve a handful of almonds, then finely crush, but don't pulverize the remaining ones.
3. In a large bowl, mix together the nuts, flours, sugar, salt, zest, and anise seed. Using your hands, mix in the butter and egg yolk until incorporated. The dough should be at the large clump stage, not a uniformly smooth dough.
4. Lay the crumbs in the pan evenly. It should be craggy, so don't sweat it.

5. Scatter reserved almonds and extra anise seed on top of cake.

6. Bake on the middle rack for 30 minutes. If the middle of the cake hasn't reached the golden-brown stage, place the pan one rack up in the oven for another 10 minutes.

7. Let cool completely and remove to a large serving platter, it might get messy.

8. When cool, dust cake with powdered sugar, if desired. The cake keeps well, wrapped in wax paper.

White Beans and Rosemary Crostini: Serves 4

I usually love white bean dips of any kind and have already established my love of bread. This is a straightforward recipe I keep handy in case of unexpected company.

Ingredients:

- 2 tablespoons olive oil, plus more for drizzling
- 3 sprigs fresh rosemary, leaves removed
- 2 cloves garlic, peeled and thickly sliced
- Two 15-ounce cans cannellini beans, drained and rinsed
- Squeeze of lemon juice
- Kosher salt and freshly ground black pepper
- Baguette, sliced

How to Make It:

1. Heat oil in a sauté pan over medium heat. Add the rosemary and garlic, and sauté until fragrant. Stir in

the beans, lemon juice and some salt and pepper.
Mash the beans with the back of a wooden spoon, but
don't mash them smooth, just break them up.

2. Stir and heat until all ingredients are incorporated
   and hot.

3. Toast the baguette slices. Serve the beans on top of
   the toasted baguette. Drizzle with olive oil if desired.

Oven-Roasted Chicken, Potatoes and Vegetables: Serves 4-5

This is a staple recipe that I grew up on. I learned it from my mom, and we lovingly call this dish simply "chicken in the oven with potatoes." It's one of my favorite autumn and winter dishes. There are tons of variations on this dish, but I find the following to be the most uncomplicated.

Ingredients:

- 2 packages boneless skinless thighs/breasts
- 2 teaspoons salt
- ½ teaspoon fresh ground pepper
- 4 sprigs fresh rosemary
- 4 sprigs fresh thyme
- 1 medium sweet onion, cut in large chunks
- 3 garlic cloves
- 1 lemon cut in quarters
- 5 tablespoons extra virgin olive oil
- 6 small Yukon gold potatoes, cut in half
- 2 carrots, peeled and cut on the bias
- ½ cup white wine

How to Make It:

1. Preheat the oven to 375-degrees.
2. Separate rosemary and thyme from stem and chop. Set aside.
3. Rinse and pat dry chicken. If mixing breasts and thighs, cut breasts in half to be roughly the same size as thighs.
4. Spray deep baking dish with non-stick spray, place chicken, onions, carrots, garlic, and lemon into the dish, fitting in potatoes, onions, garlic and carrots around the chicken. The ingredients should fit snugly into the dish.
5. Sprinkle with salt and pepper and herbs, add white wine and olive oil.
6. Cover and cook on middle rack for 25 minutes.
7. Uncover, baste and continue cooking for another 15 minutes.
8. Serve hot.

Finn's Morning-After Navajo Frybread: Serves 4

I recently tried Navajo frybread and fell in love. It's a simple fried dough recipe that can be served both savory or sweet. You can add peppers, cheese, and onions for more of a pizza effect, or you can serve with warm honey and melted butter. I'm addicted to all of it.

Ingredients:

- 2 cups canola oil for frying
- 4 cups all-purpose flour
- 3 tablespoons baking powder

- 2 tablespoons Kosher salt
- 2 ½ cups warm milk

How to Make It:

1. In a large heavy bottomed frying pan, heat 1 inch of oil to 365-degrees. Sprinkle a few drops of water. If it sizzles, you're ready.
2. In a large mixing bowl, combine flour, baking powder, salt and milk; mix well. When the dough has pulled together, form it into small balls and pat them flat.
3. Place 3 or 4 at a time into the hot oil. When the rounds begin to bubble, flip them over and cook until golden.
4. Drain on paper towels and serve hot covered in melted butter, honey or powdered sugar.

Mimi's Sunday Chicken Cutlets with Lemon Butter Sauce: Serves 2-3

I think I've been making these chicken cutlets for at least thirty years, although. I've adjusted over the years. These cutlets are such a big hit that the Tony Morrison asked for them specifically when we were neighbors in New York and she was having a meeting with the acclaimed theater and opera director Peter Sellers. The kicker to this dish is the lemon herb sauce.

Ingredients:
For the chicken:

- 1-pound boneless skinless chicken breasts

- 1 egg
- 1 cup panko crumbs
- 3/4 cup seasoned breadcrumbs
- 2 teaspoons Kosher Salt
- 2 teaspoons fresh ground pepper
- 1 teaspoon garlic powder
- 1 teaspoon onion powder
- ½ to ¾ cup canola oil for frying
- 1 handful finely chopped parsley
- ¼ to ½ cup grated Parmesan cheese
- ¼ cup half and half
- 1 cup all-purpose flour
- 1 lemon zested, juice set aside

For the sauce:

- 2 tablespoons butter
- 3 tablespoons all-purpose flour
- 2 cups low sodium chicken broth
- 1 lemon zested and juiced
- 1 tablespoon fresh chopped chives
- 1 teaspoon fresh thyme
- Kosher Salt and Black Pepper, to taste

How to Make It:
For the chicken:

1. Rinse and pat dry chicken breasts.
2. Position chicken breast in between plastic wrap or in Ziplock bags, then pound out until about ½ inch thick. Set aside. Cut into sizes that are easy to handle.

3. In a shallow bowl, add eggs, half and half, pinch of salt and pepper. Lightly beat.

4. In another dish, add Panko and seasoned breadcrumbs, lemon zest, Parmesan cheese, chopped parsley, a pinch of salt and pepper. Stir to combine.

5. In another dish, add flour, garlic and onion powder, pinch of salt and pepper. Mix to combine.

6. Add oil to a cast iron or large skillet. Heat on medium until oil bubbles and sizzles when you sprinkle in a drop of water.

7. Create an assembly line. Coat cutlet first with flour, then egg, then finish with breadcrumbs. Add to pan and cook until crispy and golden brown on each side (about 3-4 minutes each). Be careful not to burn breadcrumbs.

8. Remove from pan and let cool on a cooling rack. Season immediately with a sprinkle of salt and a squeeze of lemon juice.

9. Continue process until all cutlets are cooked. Serve immediately, or if you want, you can refrigerate and serve later simply heated in the oven.

For the sauce:

1. Melt butter in a medium saucepan and add the garlic. Sauté for 1 minute, then whisk in the flour forming a roux.

2. Cook the roux for a minute or two.

3. Gradually add in the chicken broth, whisking as you're pouring so as not to form lumps.

4. Next, add in the lemon zest and juice, chives, and thyme. Bring to a boil then allow to simmer for 5

minutes until slightly thickened. Season with salt and pepper.

5. Serve on the side with the chicken.

The Best Mashed Potatoes: Serves 4

I'm often called the "Potato Queen" by friends and family. I typically make this recipe for holidays or Sunday dinners since it can be a little heavier than weekly dinner needs. Over the years, I've tried this recipe with every type of potato imaginable, but I find Yukon gold to work the best. If you are making potatoes for a big crowd, double the recipe for a 5 lb. bag of potatoes.

Ingredients:

- 2 ½ pounds Yukon Gold potatoes
- 1 stick butter, reserve 1 tablespoon
- 2/3 cup Parmesan cheese
- ½ cup half and half
- 3 ounces diced pancetta
- 2 teaspoons salt
- 1 teaspoon fresh ground pepper
- 1 teaspoon garlic powder
- ¼ cup chopped chives or parsley for garnish
- 2/3 cup Panko breadcrumbs

How to Make It:

1. Bring a pot of salted water to a boil.
2. Peel and dice potatoes.
3. Render the diced pancetta down in a medium sauté

pan until golden but not burned. Transfer to paper towels. Retain oil rendered out of the pancetta.

4. Add potatoes to pot. Cook until tender but still firm. Drain and return in the same pot you cooked them in.

5. Add butter, half and half, Parmesan cheese, garlic powder, pancetta oil, salt, and pepper.

6. Use an immersion blender or potato masher until mixture is smooth but not gluey.

7. Add chopped chives or parsley and pancetta. Gently stir.

8. You can serve now. Or, if you are making this dish ahead, transfer mixture to a baking dish coated with non-stick spray. Cover with Panko and 1 tablespoon of butter cut in small cubes.

9. Preheat oven to 350 degrees and warm potatoes through before serving.

Baby Portobello Spinach Stuffed Mushrooms: Serves 2-3

This is another one of those childhood comfort recipes for me. My mom made these often when I was a kid, and I loved them as much then as I do now. Over the years, I've adjusted the recipe to include fresh spinach which I really think lightens the dish and adds a ton of flavor. I use whatever cheese I have on hand. You can use cheddar, mozzarella, Monterey Jack, Gruyere or Parmesan. Makes a great side dish or cocktail party appetizer.

Ingredients:

1 package fresh whole baby portobello or white mushrooms (1 1/2 to 2 inches in diameter)

1 ½ cups chopped fresh spinach (washed and carefully dried)

2/3 cup freshly grated Parmesan (or whatever cheese you want)

½ teaspoon salt

¼ teaspoon freshly ground black pepper SAVE $

½ cup Panko breadcrumbs

1 tablespoons butter or margarine, melted

How to Make It:

1. Heat oven to 425 degrees.
2. Remove stems from mushroom caps; reserve caps. Discard stems. Wipe dirt and debris gently off mushrooms using a damp paper towel. Do not rinse the mushrooms in water.
3. In large bowl, spinach, cheese, the salt and pepper and Panko.
4. Carefully spoon onto mushroom caps, mounding slightly. Place mushrooms in ungreased 17x12-inch half-sheet pan.
5. Bake 15-20 minutes until golden brown. Serve hot.

Grilled Wellfleet Oysters with Sweet Pepper Mignonette: Serves 4

I have a second-home in Provincetown and spend a great deal of time there. On one of my first visits to PTown, I was treated to Wellfleet oysters. I'll never eat another oyster again. Earthy and plump, in a perfectly sweet and salty brine, Wellfleet oysters are creamy, sweet, and mild with a crisp finish. There really is nothing like a fresh Wellfleet oyster. Shucking oysters can be an intimidating task but ask your local fishmonger to show you how to do it. That's how I learned. Once you know the trick, it's a piece of cake.

Ingredients:

- 1/4 cup rice vinegar
- 1 tablespoon freshly squeezed lime juice
- 12 oysters, scrubbed
- 2 tablespoons very finely diced red onion
- 1 small sweet pepper, seeded, finely diced with ribs removed
- 1 tablespoons finely chopped fresh chives
- 1 tablespoons finely chopped fresh cilantro
- 1 tablespoons finely chopped fresh tarragon
- Pinch of ground black pepper

How to Make It:

1. Heat the grill to high for direct grilling.
2. Stir together all remaining ingredients. Let sit at room temperature for at least 20 minutes to allow the flavors to meld.
3. Remove the tops of the oysters over a bowl, catching any of the oyster liquor that comes out. Add the liquid back to the bottom shell with the oyster.
4. Put on the grill and grill until the liquid just begins to simmer but the oysters are still a little raw in the center, about 4 minutes.
5. Carefully remove with tongs to a platter and top each oyster with a teaspoon of the mignonette and serve.

Ricotta Gnudi with Brown Butter and Sage: Serves 4

Gnudi are dumplings a bit like large gnocchi. I've seen them described as "ravioli without wrappers." However, you describe them, if prepared properly, they're light and delicious. I love how making the gnudi expanded my pasta repertoire. Give yourself plenty of time to make this dish. It easily takes a couple of hours from start to finish, and you should make the gnudi in advance, so they rest in the fridge at least overnight. Recipe adapted from The Chew's Ricotta Gnudi with Brown Butter and Sage.

https://abc.go.com/shows/the-chew/recipes/ricotta-gnudi-with-brown-butter-and-sage-michael-symon

Ingredients:

- 1-pound whole milk ricotta
- 1 cup parmesan (freshly grated, plus more for serving)
- 3/4 teaspoon nutmeg (freshly grated)
- 1-pound semolina flour (divided)
- tablespoons unsalted butter (cubed)
- 15 sage leaves
- 1/4 cup pasta water (reserved)
- Kosher salt and freshly ground black pepper (to taste)

How to Make It:

1. Line a plate with paper towels and set aside.
2. Strain the ricotta over a large bowl, discarding any excess moisture. Remove the strained ricotta to the prepared plate and allow to absorb any residual moisture. Remove ricotta to a large bowl, discarding the paper towels. Stir in the parmesan and nutmeg, and season with salt and pepper. Refrigerate until mixture is thick and beginning to firm, about 1 hour.
3. To a baking sheet, in a single layer, add half of the semolina flour on a baking sheet and place the other half in a bowl. Scoop 2 tablespoons of ricotta mixture

and place in the bowl of semolina, gently coating as you form into a ball. Place coated balls onto the prepared semolina baking sheet leaving space in between. Continue with the remaining ricotta mixture. Refrigerate, uncovered, overnight or up to 3 days, turning all prepared balls at least once for even hydration.

4. Bring a pot of salted water to a gentle boil. Carefully add gnudi to the pot. While gnudi is cooking, place a medium sauté pan over medium heat and add butter. Allow the butter to melt and become foamy, golden brown and nutty in smell, about 1-2 minutes. Add sage leaves and swirl to combine.

5. Once gnudi floats to the top of the water, transfer gnudi using a slotted spoon to butter sage mixture as well as the reserved salted water. Stir gently to coat, pour into a serving bowl and garnish with more grated parmesan on top. Serve immediately.

Grilled Lamb Chops with Caramelized Fennel and Salsa Rossa: Serves 2

I love lamb chops and grill them often. Once, I looked into my refrigerator and saw a bunch of ingredients I wasn't sure would go together. Wow do they ever! This is one of my go-to entertaining dishes when I really want to impress without breaking a sweat. Feel free to marinate the chops overnight.

For the Lamb Chops:

Ingredients:

- lamb loin chops or rack of lamb
- 2 cloves garlic minced

- 1 tablespoon olive oil
- 2 sprigs rosemary
- 1/2 tablespoon lemon zest
- 1 tablespoon lemon juice
- salt and pepper to taste

How to Make It:

1. In a plastic bag, place all ingredients but the lamb chops and salt and pepper. Mix well. Then add lamb chops and marinate overnight. Allow to come to room temperature before grilling.
2. Prepare your grill with the 2-section cooking. One part hot, one on medium to lower heat. This is key when cooking lamb because the fat will flame up and burn if you're not careful.
3. When the grill is ready, remove from the marinade and season with salt and pepper. Then place chops onto the lower temp area of the grill. You will use a thermometer to cook to the desired doneness. (125 degrees = rare, 145 = medium rare, 155 = medium). Cook the chops turning once only until the chops are 15 degrees before the desired doneness. Then move chop to the hot area of the grill to give a final sear mark. About 1 1/2 minutes per side but use your thermometer to guarantee no fail finished temperature.
4. Once at desired temp, remove from grill and allow to rest 10 minutes for juices to settle back into the chops before serving.

For the Caramelized Fennel:
Ingredients:

- 1 tablespoon extra-virgin olive oil
- 1-2 fennel bulbs, trimmed, cored, and thinly sliced
- Coarse salt and ground pepper

How to Make It:

1. In a large skillet with a tight-fitting lid, heat extra-virgin olive oil over medium-high. Add fennel, season with coarse salt and ground pepper. Cook, stirring occasionally, until mixture begins to brown, about 5 minutes. Reduce heat to medium, cover, and cook 5 to 7 minutes. Uncover, add 1 tablespoon water, and cook, stirring constantly, until golden brown and soft, 2 minutes.

For the Salsa Rossa:
Ingredients:

1. 2 large onions, finely chopped
2. 4 tablespoons olive oil
3. 2 red bell peppers
4. 1 small red chili, deseeded and chopped (remove if you don't want spice)
5. 2 cloves garlic, minced
6. 1 can chopped tomatoes
7. Salt and pepper to taste.

How to Make It:

1. Heat the oil in a saucepan and cook onions until tender.
2. Meanwhile, preheat the grill and place the peppers on a roasting pan underneath the grill.
3. Turn occasionally until their skins blister black.
4. Place in a bowl and cover with clingfilm or put in a paper bag.
5. Leave to sweat for ten minutes, then peel away the skin.
6. Discard the stalk and seeds and dice the flesh.
7. When the onions are tender, add the chili pepper, red peppers and garlic to the pan.
8. Cook for an additional 10 minutes.
9. Add the tomatoes to the pan, turn up the heat and boil for 10 minutes.
10. Taste and adjust with salt and pepper.

S'mores Homemade Graham Crackers, Marshmallows with Dark Chocolate: Serves 4-6

I'm usually not a fan of store-bought graham crackers. Making them fresh puts the graham cracker in an entirely different, and tastier, category. This is a fun dessert to make even if you aren't sitting around a campfire. This is a multi-part recipe, and I'm not going to waste space on how to assemble the S'mores. I figure you all should have that part down. The key to the marshmallow recipe is to watch your candy thermometer like a hawk. Or, just buy store bought marhmallows. That works, too! Graham cracker recipe courtesy of King Arthur Flour. Marshmallow recipe courtesy of Epicurious.com.

https://www.kingarthurflour.com/recipes/graham-crackers-recipe

https://www.epicurious.com/recipes/food/views/homemade-marshmallows-51152000

For the Graham Crackers:
Ingredients:

- 1 cup whole wheat flour, organic whole wheat flour, or whole wheat pastry flour
- 1 cup unbleached all-purpose flour
- 1/4 cup sugar
- 1/2 teaspoon salt
- 1 teaspoon cinnamon
- 1 teaspoon baking powder
- 1 large egg
- 1/4 cup vegetable oil
- 1/4 cup honey
- to 3 tablespoons milk
- additional milk for glaze
- cinnamon-sugar, optional; for topping

How to Make Them:

1. Combine the whole wheat flour, all-purpose flour, sugar, salt, cinnamon, and baking powder in a medium-sized bowl.
2. In a separate bowl, whisk the egg with the oil, honey, and 2 tablespoons milk. Stir this egg mixture into the dry ingredients until you have a fairly stiff dough, adding more milk if necessary.

3. Wrap the dough and chill it until firm, about 1 hour (or longer, if it's more convenient).
4. Preheat the oven to 300 degrees.
5. Divide the dough in half, and working with one piece at a time, knead the dough gently until it holds together. Roll the dough out about 1/16" thick onto a piece of parchment paper.
6. Transfer the rolled-out dough on the parchment paper to a baking sheet. Repeat with the second piece of dough.
7. Brush both pieces of dough with milk then sprinkle with the cinnamon-sugar, if desired.
8. Bake the sheets of dough for 10 minutes, rotating the pans after 5 minutes.
9. Remove pans from the oven and use a rolling pizza wheel or sharp knife to cut the sheets of dough into 3" x 2" rectangles; don't separate them, just cut them.
10. Return the cut crackers to the oven and continue to bake for 18 to 20 minutes.
11. Turn off the oven and open the oven door wide for 5 minutes. After the majority of the oven's heat has dissipated, shut the oven door, and let it cool down for 20 minutes with the crackers inside; this will help them become as crisp as possible.
12. Remove the crackers from the oven, transfer them to a cooling rack, and cool completely.
13. Store the crackers, well-wrapped, at room temperature for up to a week; freeze for longer storage.

For the Marshmallow:
Ingredients:

- Vegetable oil for brushing pan
- About 1 cup confectioners' sugar for coating pan and marshmallows
- 3, ¼ ounce envelopes powdered unflavored gelatin
- 1 1/2 cups granulated sugar
- 1 cup light corn syrup
- 1/4 teaspoon salt
- teaspoons pure vanilla extract

How to Make It:

1. Brush the bottom and sides of a 9-inch square baking pan with vegetable oil. Using a small, fine-mesh sieve, dust the pan generously with confectioners' sugar, knocking out any excess.

2. Put 1/2 cup water in the bowl of a stand mixer fitted with the whisk attachment. Sprinkle the gelatin into the bowl and stir briefly to make sure all the gelatin is in contact with water. Let soften while you make the sugar syrup.

3. In a heavy 3- to 4-quart saucepan, combine the granulated sugar, corn syrup, salt, and 1/2 cup water. Place over moderate heat and bring to a boil, stirring until the sugar is dissolved. Put a candy thermometer into the boiling sugar syrup and continue boiling (the mixture may foam up, so turn the heat down slightly if necessary), without stirring, until the thermometer registers 240 degrees (soft-ball stage). Remove the saucepan from the heat and let stand briefly until the bubbles dissipate slightly.

4. With the mixer on low speed, pour the hot sugar syrup into the softened gelatin in a thin stream down

the side of the bowl. Gradually increase the mixer speed to high and beat until the marshmallow is very thick and forms a thick ribbon when the whisk is lifted, about 5 minutes. Beat in the vanilla.

5. Scrape the marshmallow into the prepared pan (it will be very sticky) and use wet fingertips to spread it evenly and smooth the top. Let stand, uncovered at room temperature, until the surface is no longer sticky, and you can gently pull the marshmallow away from the sides of the pan with your fingertips, at least 4 hours or overnight.

6. Dust a cutting board with confectioners' sugar. Use a rubber spatula to pull the sides of the marshmallow from the edge of the pan (use the spatula to loosen the marshmallow from the bottom of the pan if necessary) and invert onto the cutting board. Dust the top with confectioners' sugar. Brush a long thin knife with vegetable oil and dust with confectioners' sugar to prevent sticking; continue dusting the knife as necessary. Cut lengthwise into 8 strips, then crosswise into eighths, to form a total of 64 squares. (For larger marshmallows, cut lengthwise into 6 strips, then crosswise into sixths, to form a total of 36 squares.) Coat marshmallows, one at a time, in confectioners' sugar, using a pastry brush to brush off any excess. DO AHEAD: Marshmallows can be stored, layered between sheets of wax paper or parchment in an airtight container in a dry place at cool room temperature, for 1 month.

ABOUT THE AUTHOR

Lucy J. Madison is a novelist, poet, screenwriter, and ghostwriter. In addition to her novels, her short stories, articles, and poems have appeared in dozens of literary magazines and publications nationwide. Her first feature film based on the life of Emily Dickinson is currently in production. When she's not writing, she can be found hiking, cooking, smoking the occasional cigar, and playing with her fur babies. She resides in shoreline Connecticut and Provincetown, MA. Email Lucy directly at: info@lucyjmadison.com.

WWW.LUCYJMADISON.COM